To Sherman

I am so glad
Meet you & to
share this special d

Kind Wishes

Mollie

Return to Sandy Creek

A novel by

Mollie Bickle Cardwell

Return to Sandy Creek
Copyright ©2013 by Mollie Bickle Cardwell
All rights reserved.

First Chapter Publishing
Georgetown, Texas

ISBN: 978-0-615-92772-5

This is a work of fiction. All names, characters and
incidents are the products of the author's imagination or
are used fictitiously. Any resemblance to current or local
events or to living persons is entirely coincidental.

PCN Number TXU1-884-991

Printed in The United States of America

For my family

Acknowledgments

I owe a debt of gratitude to a number of wonderful people, who encouraged and supported me in various ways:

Faye Bickle, from the first, gifted a book on writing, and continued to inquire and offer encouragement along the way.

Liz Gove and Betty Heffington, my readers, each offered enthusiastic approval of my efforts, inquiring and listening often.

Ann Inabnit loved the story from its beginning. She encouraged, praised and even embarrassed me to anyone who would listen. Ann, I'll never forget you.

My good friend, Janie Thomas, who if it is up to her, everyone will read this book.

My fellow Lake Buchanan Writer's Group members: Jean, Polly, Emma, Sarah, Iris, and Susan.

Danielle Hartman Acee and Mindy Reed, The Author's Assistant. Without your knowledge, guidance, instruction, editing, counsel and cheerleading this book wouldn't be published.

Douglas Brown, Albumartist.com. Your talent is amazing, creating the perfect cover that I could only imagine.

Mitch Cardwell, as always, providing endless technical support.

Jackie Thompson, who took a great interest, followed the progress of this book, listened, read, offered your knowledge, encouragement and proof reading expertise to the maximum! I will never be able to repay you. I am eternally grateful.

Thank you.

Chapter One

Johanna had never seen so much excitement and activity as at the boat docks along the river. There were tall stacks of cotton bales and bins of corn readied for shipping and giant piles of fresh cut timber that were being unloaded onto the water to float downstream to the mills. There were merchants and seamen and frontiersmen pulling up in their wagons, laughing and bartering among themselves, happy to see a familiar face. She was awestruck by the sophisticated gentlemen and elegantly dressed ladies who were boarding a gleaming white steamboat bound for points unknown. It was a bustling and magical place.

They loaded their wagon and team and all their worldly goods onto a flatboat just outside Memphis near Mud Island. The river would take them to lower Arkansas where they would follow the old Military Road. They would cross over the border of Arkansas, through the piney woods, down and along the old Shawnee Trail. The old cattle trails weren't used much for cattle drives anymore, but were used for other passage, as many people were moving west. The railroads that had begun to reshape the landscape had replaced the need for cattle drives and had rapidly become the preferred form of transportation. The route that they would take had been carefully planned to take them safely through inhabited areas providing access to food and supplies.

Ahead of them, on a flatboat ready to cross the river, a large family with an old Conestoga captured Johanna's attention. They had set out to ferry across the river. The Conestoga was almost too large and overloaded for the flatboat, but the river was too deep and swift to ford in the big wagon. Instead of oxen they had only cantankerous mules and seemed to be having a bad go of it.

"Father, look, they're in the water!" Johanna exclaimed.

The Conestoga had tilted off the flatboat and plunged into the water against the bank of the river. One of the boys had fallen into the water. The mother was screaming and flailing her arms. The father started running along the slippery riverbank yelling after his son. The boy's head bobbed up a few times then disappeared. Sickened, Johanna continued to gaze into the murky water as the raging current carried their flatboat on down the mighty Mississippi River, away from that dreadful scene.

Johanna and her father, Guenther Gurganis, had left their home in Shelby County looking forward to a better life and future in the West. Behind them were the memories of their home and their loving wife and mother, Elizabeth, who had fallen victim to consumption. It was a shock, after nursing the sick and infirm, and surviving the serious yellow fever epidemics unscathed, that she became so ill and died so suddenly. They were both by her bedside when she drew her last labored breath and slipped away.

Piece by piece, each item of her clothes and bedding was tossed into a fire to avoid contagion. Father and daughter stood together silently and watched as the flames curled and whisked the ashes into the night.

Guenther and Elizabeth had met late in life and were grateful for each moment they had shared. Their joy abounded when they were blessed with Johanna. After the loss of his wife, Guenther was even more determined to protect his precious daughter.

"So many things have changed," he lamented as he watched the flames.

Memphis had been decimated twice by yellow fever epidemics in the past. As many as five thousand people had died and that many or more had left the city to escape its recurrence and avoid the many people, sick and well, who continued to migrate there. They came from all over the world aboard ships arriving at the port of New Orleans. Many cities and nearby states had even banned Memphis residents from crossing their borders. The city government and coffers were floundering due to the loss of population. Smoke from industrial stacks and burn piles bellowed into the air, often making it difficult to breathe. Guenther knew they must not stay there.

Guenther was a well-known blacksmith and iron-worker in his community. He had learned his trade as a young man. Many families were still struggling with the ravages of the Civil War and depended on men like him to repair what they had at a fair price. But it was no longer the ravages of war that were the enemy. It was the ravages of disease and progress. The need for blacksmiths had begun to disappear as machines and factories replaced much of their work. But in the West there were places where a blacksmith was still needed.

Guenther thought, "We will go there."

They sold their home and Elizabeth's surrey and packed only what they could carry in the big wagon. Johanna carefully wrapped each piece of her mother's precious china, pressing it snugly into strong wooden boxes to assure safe passage. She dreamed that one day she would set a beautiful table and serve her guests on the china dishes. These fine pieces had been passed to her mother from her mother and grandmother, the only treasure left of her family.

Winter would be setting in soon. A long journey lay before them. The last items were loaded and the last box secured. After a brief pause at the gate, Guenther snapped the reins and the wagon lurched forward, scattering the few chickens left behind.

Guenther had hired a trail guide, Eli Ayers, who had made many trips west and was familiar with the rivers and wagon trails. They would travel along with other west-bound families.

Guide information posted at the telegraph office, was often accompanied by other notices. One post in particular was by a rancher who was petitioning for a blacksmith in a small community. Guenther had corresponded with the rancher to the satisfaction of both.

Destination, Texas!

Chapter Two

The Gurganis - Ayers party put ashore in Arkansas near an inland settlement named Evening Cove. Many members of the same large family made up the majority of its population. They, too, had left Tennessee to escape the epidemics and the decline of the city. They had established a thriving community, eager to sell their many goods and wares to travelers.

Under Eli's guidance, the purchasing of supplies had been postponed until after crossing the turbulent Mississippi River. From the merchants at Evening Cove they bought fodder for the horses, and staples such as corn, flour, bacon, sugar, molasses, beans, and extra canvas for the wagon. Other supplies would be replenished along the way. Eli, based on his experience, held strong to his belief, "It is unwise to overburden your wagons and your mules or oxen."

At least they had shelter that night. They soon learned it would be a many a night before they would again know the warmth of a comfortable bed.

Eli intrigued Johanna. Cooking on a campfire was a new experience for her. He could make a good meal from anything. His specialty, beans and cornbread, was supplemented by the bounty of the virgin countryside. He always brought back a squirrel or a rabbit or a deer when he went hunting. The many rivers and creeks along the way provided fish that Eli could catch with his bare hands.

Johanna quickly learned that Eli was proficient in many other tasks besides cooking. *He knows so much and is so capable*, she observed. *I wonder if this is the life he has always lived.* Secretly, she watched the movement of his muscular frame through his thin cotton shirts. Removing his hat revealed tousled, sun-kissed hair against smooth bronzed skin. "He is very handsome," she concluded.

There had been reports along the way of Indian renegades who had stolen livestock and burned homes and farm buildings. A confrontation with Indians was an event that Eli hoped to avoid. He wasn't likely to forget a past experience while scouting with a cavalry regiment. An arrow in his thigh almost cost him his leg. Three soldiers lost their lives that day.

After the Indian wars in Texas, most tribe members had been moved onto reservations. The rest caused little or no trouble, but on occasion, an angry raiding party could still prove to be dangerous. Johanna was fearful of being kidnapped and raped by Indians, but the stories of cannibalism among some of the earlier tribes were even more terrifying. She put her trust into Eli to keep her and her father safe. *He would know what to do if necessary*, she reasoned.

The weather proved to be another threat. A thunderstorm often meant seeking shelter and safety under the wagons. Sometimes it meant spending an entire night huddled underneath them. The remedy seldom kept them dry, nor were they able to sleep. It also meant lying with snakes and scorpions. Johanna couldn't decide which was worse. Even when the skies cleared, the morning often brought the dangerous task of pushing and pulling the wagons from the mud.

Following along the Old Military Road to the border of Texas, they cut across to catch the old Shawnee Trail route. It took them along newly laid railroad tracks that ran for miles and miles. A train engine's whistle pierced the early morning air as it charged down the tracks pulling only a caboose. A white-haired, uniformed man stood on the platform waving as they passed. The train was traveling in the same direction as their group. As Eli calmed the horses, Johanna found herself wishing she were on board and wondered, *Why can't we travel to Texas by train?* Instead, she sat on the hard seat of their wagon as it wound through the ruts and stumps of the dense pine forests of northeast Texas.

Their numbers dwindled as other families met the end of their passage and split away from the small group. With a twinge of envy, Johanna witnessed the happiness among them as many were reunited with family members who had come years earlier. Her only joy was the knowledge that their journey's end was just a few days away.

They were going to cross the Colorado River at Gleason's Crossing. The many rivers and creeks of Texas had offered uneventful passage, but this river was deep and swollen from storms days earlier. The water surged out of its banks and was full of tree branches and debris. Eli recommended that they wait overnight until the water receded. "We'll take the crossing in two trips," He explained. "We'll take one with the wagon and oxen, and the other with the remaining animals. I'll cross with the wagon. Johanna and Guenther, you'll cross with the animals." This proved to be a wise decision.

The ferries tilted and swayed and dipped as the muddy water rushed over the floorboards. Briefly caught in an eddy, Johanna's skirts swirled around her ankles. Guenther lost his footing, but strong ropes tied around his wrists saved his life.

Their last hurdle was to ascend the muddy riverbank at the landing. With the help of pulleys and ropes and their mighty oxen, Johanna and Guenther pushed the wagon from behind while Eli expertly guided the oxen up and over the steep embankment.

Johanna was relieved they were once again on level ground and that the river crossing was safely behind them. "Before we continue," Eli said, "I want to check the wagon and livestock thoroughly. Take the time to dry and rest before we proceed."

Johanna was anxious to move forward, but knew better than to protest.

Once Eli was comfortable that everything was secure and undamaged, the group resumed their journey.

They had traveled only a short distance, however, when Eli gave the signal to stop. They had come upon an abandoned camp. "So near the landing, yet unknown to the ferry operator?" Eli wondered out loud. He scrutinized the area, stating with near certainty their good fortune. "I think we have missed the Indian renegades, here! How is it the ferry operator knew nothing of this camp?" Time would not allow Eli to cross back over the river. The question would go unanswered.

It had been several months and the boggy, bumpy roads, the heat, the rain, and swarming mosquitoes were nearly behind them. Johanna hoped there would be less rain and fewer rivers to cross. Her father noted how the landscape had changed from pine trees and yaupon to noble oaks, mesquites and juniper. Guenther knew the trip had been hard on his daughter, but believed they were headed to a better life.

Although they were approaching the Hill Country he arranged to spend a few days in the capital of Texas before heading northwest.

Recently built by a wealthy cattle baron, a lavish hotel greeted them. The exterior was grand, the interior was opulent; green velvet drapes framed the windows. Glancing into the dining room as they crossed the lobby, Johanna could see that meals were served on fine china and white tablecloths. There was finally a clean dry bed with starched, ironed sheets awaiting her in her own room.

Austin was a busy, noisy place. The aroma of fresh baked pastries and coffee filled the air. There were many things to see and do and Austin was much more refined than Johanna had expected. She had heard stories of cattle being driven through the streets of the city. She had heard about fights between drunken cowboys ending in gun battles right in front of the jail. She also heard many good stories, among them the battles at the Alamo and about the Father of Texas, Stephen F. Austin, for whom the capital was named.

"I could stay here forever!" she exclaimed.

Guenther had business in Austin. Although he had a commitment to the rancher, he sought out a land broker in order to confirm rumors of partial land grant sales. Many immigrants had settled in the state. Their farms and settlements were sometimes unsuccessful. Some of the forfeited land was being divided and sold or rented in smaller tracts. Gunther's ambition was to establish himself once again as a good blacksmith. While he did not want to profit from the misfortune of others, he was interested in information about land ownership. After he visited the land broker, he went to the telegraph office and sent word to the rancher that he and his daughter would be arriving in a few days.

They would no longer need the strong lumbering oxen, so Guenther traded them for much faster mules. He replenished their supplies, attended to a few wagon repairs, and prepared for their final days of travel.

Johanna visited local shops and wandered about the city, stopping at a dressmaker's shop. Her father had arranged for a new dress and hat. While selecting her fabric, she entertained the other women with the adventures of their trip. As she strolled down Congress Avenue and approached the hotel, she imagined she was an elegant lady, like those at the steamboat on the Mississippi, and the hotel was her mansion.

A very special dinner was planned to celebrate their last night in Austin. When Johanna learned that Eli would be joining them, she was disappointed to hear this would be their last night with him, as well. She did not sense that he paid her any special attention during their journey, but she hoped her new dress and sophisticated hairdo would make a permanent impression on him. They had a delightful dinner of quail and roasted potatoes and baked apples with cinnamon and sugar. Guenther ordered a bottle of wine and even allowed his daughter to join them in a toast to their guide. Many toasts later, they ended their evening and their long journey together.

ଧ୍ୟଓଃ

Just before daylight a quiet knock on her door awakened Johanna.

"Eli!" His silhouette filled her doorway.

Johanna couldn't hide her surprise.

Stepping closer, silently looking deep into her eyes, there was an expression on his face that she'd never seen. His lip quivered as he attempted, but failed, to speak. She leaned forward to hug him, but suddenly she could feel his heart pounding in his chest as he lifted her off her feet, pressing her body firmly against his. To her astonishment, he put his mouth on hers. That kiss, Johanna's first, would be burned into her memory forever. He abruptly released her and hurried away, exiting a nearby stairwell. She stood breathless, looking at the empty hallway.

Johanna stepped back into her room, closed the door, and sat on the bed. She tried to understand what had just happened. As much as she wanted to believe that a future with Eli would be possible, she had to accept reality.

Eli's life was that of a frontiersman. His days were filled with pushing the country westward. She did not think she would want a home and family with someone who would be absent for months on end.

As Eli saddled his horse and prepared to leave Austin, he wondered if he had done the right thing. "She's too young." He told himself for the thousandth time. He spent the entire journey resisting his desires and pretending he had no interest in that pure, beautiful girl. He knew he probably shouldn't have kissed her, but also knew that he was doing the right thing by leaving.

Eli Ayers left the hotel in Austin that morning at dawn. He was headed to Gleason's Crossing.

Chapter Three

The wagon bumped along the trail (Guenther did not possess Eli's skills as a trail driver). Johanna was day-dreaming about Eli. She touched her lips and imagined that there had been more than a kiss between her and Eli. She blushed at the thought. *I wish I'd known of his interest in me,* she thought, *I would have tried harder to engage him.* There were boys in Tennessee who showed an interest in her, but she rebuffed them. She knew how to discourage a boy, but had no knowledge how to encourage one.

I hope I get to see Eli again someday, somehow, she mused. *Father was nice to him, but I know he would never approve of a frontiersman as a suitor.* The early morning visit would remain her secret.

The land continued to rise gradually as they edged higher toward the hills. The mules struggled with the weight of the wagon, but Guenther knew they were better suited to the terrain than the oxen. The loamy soil behind them had turned into limestone, granite, and sand. Hot and dry, it appeared to be better for ranching than farming. This boded well for a blacksmith.

"What do you think of the countryside?" Guenther asked his daughter.

Johanna was lost in her thoughts and had not noticed her surroundings. "It's nice," she responded absently.

"The Colorado River runs through the area, as well as the Llano and many creeks and springs," he told her. "I think we will be happy here." Rumors of failed farms and land sales by earlier settlers were confirmed by the land broker and were becoming a reality to Guenther as he observed the countryside around them. They passed by several abandoned farms and empty barns, and overgrown pastures with no sign of life or livestock.

The rancher had provided Guenther with a good map and reliable directions. In less than a day they had made their way to an encampment near Sandy Creek. There, they would spend the last night of their journey with other wagons and tents that lined the creek under the shade of tall pecan and oak trees. Many campfires were burning and furniture placed around the wagons left the impression that many of the travelers had been there for a long time. Their approach brought curious stares from some and greetings from others. It was apparent that some of the occupants were on hard times and some perhaps a bit unsavory.

Johanna knew they each had a story and wondered what it might be. *Has the lure of the West brought them here or a tragedy, like our own?* She pondered.

Her father was speaking to a few of the people in German, but Johanna did not understand the language well enough to know what was being said.

This is an eerie, depressing place. I'm glad our stay will be brief, she thought. Although there had been danger, and at times boredom, on their cross-country journey, at no time did she feel despair.

Guenther was as restless as his daughter and slept fitfully, waiting for a ray of sun to burst through the heavy morning clouds. When morning came, fires were already stoked and burning. The aroma of coffee from another traveler's pot filled his nostrils and urged him out of the wagon. Grateful for a cloudy day to travel, Guenther hurried for an early start.

They were on the way quickly. This was the last day of their journey. Guenther was conflicted: anxious for what lay ahead and sad for what lay behind.

ഇരുൽ

It was easy to see how Sandy Creek got its name. Pure, clean sand stretched in either direction as far as the eye could see. The water was cool, clear and shallow. The banks of the creek were etched where flash floods occurring through the centuries had left their story. There was evidence that many animals visited the creek, leaving their prints where they came to drink. The road narrowed to a single lane bridge. As her father took the wagon and team across the bridge, Johanna held up her skirt and waded into the cool water, carrying her shoes and stockings. The sand squished up between her toes. She washed her face, allowing the cool water to run through her fingers. Her reflection looked back at her as she watched tiny minnows dart through the water.

"Hello, Sandy Creek."

Chapter Four

As they entered the town, Guenther slowed the mules to a halt. Both Guenther and Johanna were surprised to discover that the community was so well established. There was a rock building, a livery stable and blacksmith. Opposite was a hotel and general store. The rock building appeared to be a school or church. A portion of the street in front of the hotel had been layered with bricks. A large rock cistern was located behind the hotel. Several people were gathered under the walkway in front of the hotel and adjoining building. A sign over the hotel read, "Cain Hotel." A similar sign with the Cain name hung over the general store. To his own surprise, maybe from relief or exhaustion, laughter burst forth from Guenther, "There is no doubt about who is the owner of this town. Hopefully, there will be a room for us!"

Sara Cain, the hotel's proprietor, was overjoyed when she learned her guests were the new blacksmith and his daughter. "We've been expecting you!" She called for her husband, "Abel, the new blacksmith is here." Guenther was relieved that their arrival was expected and met with such enthusiasm. The rancher had undoubtedly communicated his plan to the community. "You will be able to stay here until you find a home," Sara insisted. "We have a suite available with a drawing room and bedroom. That should be perfect for you and Johanna. We serve two meals a day." She squeezed Johanna as she spoke. Guenther was very pleased to learn of these accommodations. Johanna held back tears of relief brought by the warmth of Sara Cain's hug, a long-missed motherly gesture. "I know you must be hungry. Come with me, I have leftovers from supper." Sara said.

ജൗ

Johanna pulled the covers over herself. The bed felt cool and clean. *No more sleeping in the wagon, no more cooking on a campfire*, she thought with pleasure. She watched the fresh curtains as they rose and fell in the cool breeze. She was restless, but felt safe listening to her father breathing as he slept soundly in the adjoining room.

She ached as thoughts of her mother filled her mind. She suddenly remembered Sara Cain's hug. Her mind raced on to Eli's firm embrace, and the waves of excitement that had rushed through her as his lips met hers. "Eli," she whispered. She hoped that someday she would find someone like Eli, brave and strong and handsome. She hoped for a marriage like that of her parents. *I hope we meet again.*

She had blossomed into a young woman over the past few years. She touched her breasts, curious about her body. There were so many unanswered questions. "Mother," she whispered. That familiar lump rose in her throat again as she waited quietly for sleep.

∞୧୦∞

The sounds of the day awakened her. She set straight up in the bed, looking for a clock. Aromas from the kitchen wafted through the hotel. Johanna's stomach growled. She dressed quickly and rushed downstairs to find her father, who was visiting with Sara.

The Cain Hotel was the center of activity in the little flourishing community. A cafe was part of the hotel and the general store was attached through a doorway. Her father and Sara Cain were in the cafe along with several other guests. Abel Cain was behind the hotel desk putting mail into slots. Delivery was made there twice a week. The residents of the community came to collect their mail, often staying for lunch or dinner or stopping by the general store for supplies or a visit.

"Our former blacksmith, Bob, was injured when a horse kicked him," Sara explained. "He couldn't work anymore, so he packed up and went back east. We bought the blacksmith shop to help him out. He did some of his farrier work out at the ranches. The ranchers hope for the same arrangement with you."

"I'm sorry to hear of his troubles," Guenther said. "I hope to serve the community well."

There was to be a meeting of the ranchers, the Cain's, and Guenther. "Many of the ranchers will be coming into town for the fall festival," Sara explained. "They want to meet you. I'm sure both you and Johanna will enjoy the festivities."

છા૭ઝ

Sara sent Dodge Blackburn to help Guenther move their belongings into the hotel. Items they didn't need immediately were locked away in the livery stable. Their mules and horses were turned out into a pen behind the livery. Special care was taken to move the boxes of china into the hotel. "Please be careful with those boxes." Johanna implored. She was very protective of her mother's china.

Dodge had helped build the hotel and other buildings belonging to the Cain's. He was as committed to Sara and Abel as if they were his own family. The truth was that Sara and her family were the only real family he'd ever known. He had known Sara since she was a girl. Her father had trusted him so much that he had Dodge accompany her to the Hill Country after her marriage to Abel Cain.

Dodge was one of the many homeless youngsters who hung around the Galveston docks, taking whatever work or food he could find or steal. One day the boy appeared at the back door of the Freeze General Store. Sara's parents had taken him in, and given him a home.

৪০০৪

Johanna woke up to the noise of the men working on the platform for the fall festival. She was excited about the dance and was counting down the days. She watched them through the window of the dining room where she had joined Sara Cain. She savored every bite of Sara's breakfast, but was eager to be outside, involved in the activities.

As she strolled from the hotel to her father's blacksmith shop, she noticed a banner that had been raised above and across the street. It read: Annual Fall Festival September 26. "Just two weeks," she sighed. She went into the shop and handed her father the lunch she had brought him. "A festival will be so much fun," she said.

"Maybe there will be people from the school there, people your own age," Guenther responded.

In anticipation of the festival, Johanna returned to her room to unpack her trunk and hang her dresses. She selected her new dress to wear to the festival and hung it and her petticoats near the window to freshen in the autumn air.

She pulled one more item from the trunk: a small leather purse with a tiny gold clasp and tooled flower design. Her mother's scent filled the room when she opened it. The purse contained a jeweled powder box, lip rouge, and a dainty bottle of pleasant lilac fragrance. Elizabeth's wedding ring and that small pouch; the only personal belongings withheld from the fire. With both hands, she gently held the purse longingly to her cheek.

"Mother," she whispered.

ŏᴖᴄᴣ

The building that had looked like a school or church was just that, both a school and a church. The school went to tenth grade, which Johanna had completed the previous year. Students from the surrounding area attended the school, which was much larger than the typical one-room schoolhouse in most homestead communities. The church was ministered by Reverend Luke Matthews, whom everyone knew was handy with a hammer, and in the midst of the men working on the platform.

The Reverend Matthews was always present for projects in the community. He was the first person to show up when volunteers were needed to build the county roads, always present to help build a house, or to raise a barn. He conducted Sunday services, weddings and funerals for much of the surrounding area, and was loved by everyone. He had come to the Hill Country when an uncle died and left him a small farm. Luke owned some livestock and a small pecan orchard that he thrashed each year. He managed to earn a small livelihood from his farm, which allowed him to follow his true calling as a country preacher. He would have little or no income otherwise, as there were simply no funds in the modest congregation to offer him a salary. His compensation consisted of fresh baked pies and bread, canned goods, a chicken, or an occasional invitation to supper.

ഇൗ൪

Johanna left the hotel. Sara had asked her to fetch her father for dinner. However, instead of being at the blacksmith shop, she found him at the platform nailing the last few boards into place. When he stood up, a handsome young man shook his hand. "Thanks for your help, Guenther. I'd never hear the end of it if we didn't finish in time," the young man said.

"It was my pleasure." Guenther looked up and saw Johanna staring at them. "Come, let me introduce you to my daughter."

Johanna was suddenly self-conscious and smoothed her hair with her hands. She was curious about this young preacher and was happy to make his acquaintance.

⊱⊰

Even before the ranchers came to town for the festival, Guenther wanted to begin the process of becoming a fellow landowner. Abel had introduced him to Ephraim Fields, a land agent who had knowledge of a small tract of land that backed up to Sandy Creek.

"There's plenty of water on the place, a good well, and an established peach orchard," Fields told Guenther. Working for the land corporation, it was Mr. Field's job to liquidate vacant farms.

Guenther had heard that land agents were not always trustworthy and often had reputations for separating unsuspecting immigrants and settlers from their money. However, he doubted Abel would turn him over to a reprobate.

Although the land was as the agent had described, the house was in total disrepair. He and Johanna would have to remain in the hotel until it was livable again. It would be a big step and would require some serious thought and the assistance of a lawyer. The apartment above the blacksmith shop would be sufficient for him, but not for Johanna. She needed a proper home, but one day she would find a husband and he would be left with a big place he didn't need. Mr. Fields would have to wait for an answer.

Johanna followed Sara Cain around the general store while she prepared a purchase order for the drummer, who frequently stopped by the store. She had remained at the hotel while her father rode out with Mr. Fields.

"He sells land and his name is Fields," Johanna chuckled to Sara, quickly covering her mouth with her hand.

Fabrics from muslin to silk, lace, threads, and other sundries filled the bins. Millinery and household items, pots and pans, medicines, and home canned vegetables lined the shelves. Barrels of dried beans, ground meals, and flour sat on the floor, creating walkways between them. The store was stocked wall to wall, from the floor to the ceiling.

A stagecoach stopped through two times a week and dropped off supplies and mail and frequently a traveler en route to or from Austin. Johanna enjoyed helping put the mail into the slots.

"Mrs. Cain, may I work here? At least until we find a home and move out of the hotel?"

"Abel and I could surely use some help, Johanna. With the festival just a few weeks away, we'll be having additional guests. I have heard the governor himself may stop through here. You can start right now. We will teach you everything you need to know."

Johanna spent the remainder of the day cleaning and helping Sara Cain, anxiously awaiting her father's return. She had good news to share at supper that evening, a good reason to celebrate.

Chapter Five

The days passed slowly while Johanna waited impatiently for the festival. Finally, early in the afternoon on the 26th, the real preparations began.

A group of ranch hands from the Terrell ranch arrived to start the fires. Mike Terrell had always supplied the meat for the festival, while everyone else who attended brought other foods and homemade beer. The ranch hands would cook a steer, a goat and a hog, cattle-drive style, on open fires. They used a mix of oak, pecan, and mesquite woods to create the best combination of smoke and slow cooking. The meat would be turned and cooked for hours with seasonings added as it cooked. The aromatic blend of the smoke and spices permeated the entire community.

Local residents slowly began to fill the streets, and wagons loaded with happy families appeared from every direction. Tables and benches lined the streets, with the platform right in the middle of all the activities. Canopies were hung to provide afternoon shade, and lanterns were swung for light in the evening. A band had assembled near the platform. There would be music and dancing.

Fresh and clean, Johanna slipped into her petticoats and dress. She curled her hair and pulled it up off her neck with a ribbon. She touched her lips lightly with her mother's rouge and pinched her cheeks really hard so they would be pink. Then she gently pressed the slightest bit of powder onto her clear, smooth skin. Filled with anticipation, she started down the stairs, relieved to find her father in the lobby. Arm in arm they exited the hotel and entered their new world.

The festivities had begun. The band was playing lively German music, people were dancing on the platform, children were playing games in the street, dominoes and card games were underway at the tables. A cart was piled with quilts, along with handmade baskets, homemade pies and canned goods that were all displayed, awaiting the auction that was held each year. Laughter and joy filled the air.

A sight to behold, the men from the Terrell ranch thundered up in a cloud of dust, waving their hats in the air, riding full speed all the way from the ranch. Mike Terrell was in the lead as if he was still a young man, leaping off his horse before it even stopped. The others followed suit. Everyone yelled and greeted them happily. Guenther and Johanna hung back a bit, waiting for the crowd to settle.

Abel Cain stepped beside Guenther as Mike Terrell approached. "Mike, this is Guenther Gurganis. This is his daughter, Johanna. He is the new blacksmith. This is Mike Terrell."

Sara Cain introduced Johanna to many people that evening. Some of the people she already knew from visits to the general store or from their names on the mail slots. Eager to meet other young people her age, Johanna was disappointed to learn there were none. A young man, who had ridden in with Mr. Terrell, had dismounted and was striding toward them. His hat was pulled down over his face, his duster brushing the toes of his boots.

B.G. had noticed Johanna and was unable to take his eyes off her. She was the most beautiful girl he'd ever seen. He had overheard that the new blacksmith from Tennessee had arrived with a daughter, but he had never expected her to be so beautiful. He made his way through the crowd that surrounded Sara Cain, as she waved him over to her. "B.G., this is Johanna Gurganis. Her father is our new blacksmith. Johanna, this is B.G. Steven. He lives and works with Mike Terrell."

B.G. nodded his head, "Very pleased to meet you, ma'am." Johanna's heart skipped a beat as he raised his head to look at her from beneath the brim of his hat. After he shed his hat and duster, he took her hand and guided her to the dance floor.

B.G. and Johanna circled the floor dance after dance, neither of them speaking. Johanna hoped that he wouldn't ask her a question, fearful that she couldn't speak. Her mind was racing. She could feel the heat from his body. She dared not look into his eyes, lest he might read her thoughts. Johanna's sweet fragrance and the soft feel of her body, light as a feather, mesmerized him. His chest felt tight as he wished the evening would never end. But end it would, for B.G. was supposed to ride fence that night, and had to return to the ranch before nightfall.

഻ഝ

Cattle rustlers, Indian raids, migrants, itinerants; the stock was guarded day in and day out to prevent rustling or theft. With wire cutters and a wagon many calves could be hauled away overnight. The barbed wire fence that had painstakingly been built around the Terrell ranch pastures was little deterrent against a large enough opening cut through the wire in the dark of night. Rustlers would herd cattle through the cut. Others would kill a steer on the spot and haul away the meat, leaving the carrion for the buzzards and coyotes, only to be discovered when the offender was long gone. Suspicion often rested against the residents at the encampment down by the creek. People there were on hard times. Dangerous Indian renegades were another story. The hands on duty carried rifles and pistols, or, if needed, a lantern on a moonless night. Although B.G. was practically a son, he took his turn riding fence the same as the other cowboys. That night, he would be thinking about Johanna Gurganis. He left the festival, but took his shortcut along the north fork, and down through the cedar break and out across the range. Filled with excitement, he rode hard and fast, his heart bursting.

"How can I see her again?"

Johanna could think of nothing but B.G. Steven. She lost all interest in the festival after his departure. Later, she lay awake for a very long time. The events of the evening lingered in her mind. Looking out at the night sky she saw a shooting star explode through the darkness. *B.G., are you my shooting star? Eli, is that you?* she thought. Her father was going to the Terrell Ranch the next morning. Johanna devised a plan.

The day began early in the hotel kitchen. Johanna was already there when Sara came downstairs. "My goodness, you've started early." Responding to Sara's greeting, Johanna quickly explained her plan. Aware of the evening that Johanna and B.G. had shared, and aware of Guenther's scheduled visit to the Terrell Ranch, Sara was excited for Johanna. Her wish that those two would become friends was coming true right before her eyes.

Horse saddled and ready to go, Guenther came into the hotel to say goodbye.

"Father, may I join you on your trip to the Terrell ranch? I would love to see the ranch and the ranch house and I would love to see Sandy Creek again, this time on horseback."

"I'll saddle Pebble." Seldom able to refuse his daughter, Guenther returned to the stable. Johanna was pleased her plan had worked.

A proud Spanish Andalusian, named for his spotty gray coat and white stockings, Pebble had been Elizabeth's horse. He had pulled her surrey. He had been her steed. Elizabeth loved him and trusted him with Johanna. Agile and spirited, he was also gentle. Johanna loved him, too. She had spent many hours working and training him alongside her mother. More than just her horse, Pebble was her friend and companion, and she looked forward to the ride out to the Terrell ranch on a crisp fall morning.

Johanna quickly dressed for riding in pants, a jacket, and her riding boots. She pulled her hair up under her hat, grabbed a scarf and hurried out the door. Guenther was stunned at the resemblance to her mother. Suddenly his daughter had become a woman.

Chapter Six

With his head resting against his saddle, Eli Ayers caught a glimpse of a shooting star in the western sky. He wondered if perhaps Johanna was awake, also witnessing the beauty blazing through the blackness. Having received no news of their further travels, he wondered if they had made it to their final destination. *Did Guenther make contact with the rancher? Was the community what they'd expected?* He hoped that when he finally made it back to Tennessee someone there would have news of the Gurganis family. His body stirred as he remembered the longing he felt that last morning. He remembered Johanna's soft lips and warm sweet breath. He had stolen that kiss, the only one that had ever had any meaning, knowing he would never see her again. The memory had sustained him through some troubling events since he left her and her father in Austin, Texas.

Off the trail, he had hidden for hours in the dense brush on the bank of the Colorado River, kneeling silently, watching the peculiar activities at Gleason's Crossing. The Indian camp was empty, but there was evidence that it had been occupied again. Suspicious about this odd activity, he was curious that their own party hadn't been robbed when they passed through there. However, at the time, there had been no reports of travelers being harmed or robbed. Remaining vigilant, he didn't build a fire that night. He fought sleep, but was soon startled completely awake by voices. He rubbed his eyes, as he could hardly believe what he saw. The light of the moon on that clear night revealed Indians moving around the ferry, entering and exiting the building. To his disbelief, the operator and another man were there among them, apparently unharmed and unafraid. Then he saw one of the Indians remove his feathered headdress and hair. *A white man disguised as an Indian?* Eli wondered. Then it finally all made sense. The camp was a decoy, which explained some of its questionable appearance, and also explained why the ferry operator didn't mention anything about Indians or the camp. *What were they up to?* Rather than attempt anything alone, Eli rode for the nearest sheriff's office.

Eli's pounding on the door at the sheriff's office finally produced a sleepy deputy. After quickly explaining the activity he had witnessed, he and the deputy went to rouse the sheriff. Eli proceeded to tell them the whole story about how he and the Gurganis family had crossed the river and found the strange, abandoned camp. He told how his curiosity had forced him to return to the crossing on his way back to Tennessee. He hadn't been able to understand why the operator didn't warn them of that camp or the Indians, about which he would have surely known. Listening carefully, the sheriff and his deputy began to put together the clues. Attacking travelers would bring them too close to their victims, allowing their identification. It explained everything and made sense of the recent incidents that had been reported and blamed on Indian renegades. Empty homes, farms, and businesses had been their target. Several barns and homes had been burned and animals killed. All of these tactics had been to divert blame toward the Indians. Based on reports, rustling and theft were the objective. Many cattle had been reported stolen. Homes of families away temporarily had been robbed of money and valuables. A posse would be necessary to overpower that group, not knowing how many there were. They were pretending to be Indians. Wise old Lone Wolf himself, an Indian from Eli's past, could not have been so sly.

Deputized, Eli joined the sheriff, the deputy, and several other men and set out for Gleason's Crossing. By late afternoon they approached the landing. As Eli had done before, they watched through the trees and brush waiting for nightfall. They, too, witnessed the peculiar activity that Eli had reported. They split up and took the group by surprise by creeping up on foot to the backside of the building. The others charged up on their horses. Sur-rounded, there was no way to escape. The skirmish result-ed in the capture and arrest of the ferry operator, his brother and the rest of the unscrupulous band of ne'er-do-wells.

Proud that his suspicions had been correct and that his actions had served to protect the safety and prop-erty of many people, Eli resumed his journey home, where once again he would guide another group to Texas, or maybe to California or to Oregon. For now, he would be following the old Shawnee Trail up through the piney woods along the Military Road through Arkansas and across the mighty Mississippi River back to Tennessee.

Chapter Seven

Sara Cain would miss Johanna's help that day. After the festival there were a lot of extra chores to do, but she was happy for those two young people to be together. She was glad that Guenther had agreed to let Johanna accompany him to the Terrell ranch.

She remembered her own romance with Abel and her immediate attraction to him when he entered her father's general store. He was recently new to America from England, and she found his accent charming. Their courtship continued for a year before Abel proposed, but their wedding was planned quickly. They'd received a land grant and were moving to the Hill Country to open a general store there. Her parents would join them after their retirement. Sara's father had funded and helped them build and open the store, returning to Galveston afterward.

Dodge Blackburn had accompanied Sara at the request of her father. He was loyal to her father, but his love for Sara ran much deeper than she or anyone would ever know. If nothing else, he considered himself her protector. Because he loved her, he worked tirelessly at the store and in the community. He had no expectation that she would ever return his love. She loved Abel.

Sara and Abel had been married for eight years when the Gurganis family arrived at the Cain hotel. She was convinced that the burden of the store and cafe and finally the hotel had prevented her from conceiving a child. Life was hard in the country. Water had to be hauled inside from the water pump that Abel had installed outside the kitchen. Pitchers of water were carried to the guest rooms for bathing. Wood had to be chopped and carried to the woodpile almost daily. Laundry was done outside in large pots over open flames. Each of the businesses had evolved from the other and had become more than antici-pated. She was grateful for Dodge and his tireless work, for it was difficult to find other reliable help in their remote area. She was also grateful for Johanna now, and hoped that she would continue to work at the store and hotel.

Abel wanted children, many children. Sara knew he was very disappointed that their love hadn't brought forth a child. Each month, she could see it in his face. His passion was powerful. He loved her deeply and was certain their love would bring a child soon. So tired herself, Sara often wished Abel weren't so passionate, that sometimes he would be too tired to reach for her, but he seldom was. Truly fearful of delivering a baby without a doctor or her mother present, Sara was secretly relieved she hadn't become pregnant. Besides, how could she run the business with children at her feet? There were other ladies in the community whom Sara knew would come to help her. She had never seen a baby born, although one had been born to a local family a few years ago. That mother's screams could be heard even at the hotel and were firmly imprinted in her memory. She knew her mother would try to come, but leaving her father to run their store alone would be a difficult decision. In each of her letters she pleaded with them to sell their store and come to the Hill Country.

Sara and Abel had lived in a small room at the back of the general store. Once the upstairs had been completed, they moved up there and Dodge moved into the small room. They built the kitchen for themselves, but frequently passengers on the stagecoach asked for food, so the kitchen became a cafe and Sara began to cook more and more. A very good cook, she enjoyed the compliments from the guests, but she soon needed help.

A stroke of luck brought them Etta Grant, whose husband, Daniel, was a retired, crippled Buffalo Soldier. His attempt at tenant farming had failed. Forty acres was not enough land to make a successful crop. Unable to do all the work himself, unable to afford to hire help, and having no children, he eventually gave up. Etta took over the kitchen and developed a reputation for the hotel as having the best bread and pies anywhere.

Dodge and Abel added on to the building and the hotel was born. The blacksmith and his family moved to the area and built their home, shop, and stable. In just a few years the community had grown to its current size. A stagecoach had begun stopping twice a week. The residents in the area built the church, which was also used for the school.

Petitions had been started to name and incorporate the town. Slow to infiltrate the sparsely populated Hill Country, it was rumored that a railroad was expected to lay tracks nearby, which would assure the success of the community.

Although there was a doctor an hour away, another of Sara's dreams was to persuade a doctor to open an office. There were high hopes and big plans for the future of their little settlement.

Sara was worried about her parents. If she hadn't needed Dodge Blackburn so much herself, she would've tried to send him back to Galveston. She worried about Dodge, too. Surely someday he might like to make a life of his own. He was a handsome, kind man. She didn't know of anything he couldn't do. He would be a good husband to some lucky lady. He had always been so kind and loyal to her and her family. She felt guilty, because they couldn't have accomplished all they had without his help.

Chapter Eight

Always fearful and very private about her life, Etta clung to Daniel, so much so that when she first began working at the hotel, he stayed there with her every day for a long time. Only when she finally began to feel secure and safe, did he bring her and leave for the day. There was far more to her story than being married to such a fine man. That Buffalo Soldier was much more than that to her.

Originally from Louisiana, Etta's family came to central Texas with their owner. As a young woman her mother became a house servant, and eventually, something more to her master. Her husband, Etta's father, was sent away. She had more babies, but they were always taken away after birth. She didn't want them taken away, she wanted to keep them and love them like she did her other children, but had nothing to say in the matter. Many times, Etta would see tears in her mother's eyes, but was much too young to understand.

She and her children were treated especially well, as long as she was discreet and avoided the lady of the house. Etta remembered they were all sent out of their house whenever the master came in the evenings. The master's visits were brief, but when he left, her mother would always cry. Etta knew that she did not want the master to come to her house when she grew up. Whatever he did or said to her mother must hurt very badly.

When they came to Texas, she and all of her family lived in tents until their owner's house was completed. Then several small houses were built for them to share.

There was rumor and talk all over the country about emancipation. *Will we actually be free? What will we do? Where will we go?* Having no man, the only thing they knew to do was to stay right where they were and hope the master would continue to take care of them.

Etta didn't understand what war was. She knew a lot of the men left for a fight. Those who stayed, like their master, began to treat them differently. Then one day the master told them they could not live there anymore. Only a few men would be allowed to stay to work the fields and stock. If they wanted to live in the small houses they had to pay rent.

People who had ignored them, or who were at least kind to them in the past, were now mean and sometimes even spit on them. When the war was over things continued to get worse. Etta and her siblings hadn't been allowed to go to school. Now it was something they could never hope for. Their mother took a job cleaning the house of a wealthy lady in town.

For Etta and her family, freedom was much worse than their life before. One day everything got dramatically worse. It was rumored that a black man had killed a white woman. It seemed everyone in the town, the whole county, went crazy. The white folks were fighting among themselves, some trying to protect the blacks and some demanding the opposite.

A loud mob formed and the man suspected of killing the white woman was lynched without even a trial. Lynching had become common and everyone was equally at risk, black or white.

The frenzy went on. Vigilante justice seemed to rule the county. Dejected men, who were angry over the outcome of the war, took the law as they saw it, into their own hands, lynching several men. Some of them were more respectable than others. Some were reckless and dangerous, taking advantage of people's fears. Law and order was scantily enforced.

Finally, because of the killing of the white woman, everyone became convinced that all the blacks must go. Warnings went out to all blacks that they must leave the county or be killed.

Etta's mother took her children and everything they could carry and left the county. The last kind act of their master was to give them a wagon, which they loaded quickly and left.

They had no idea where to go or where they were. They just stayed on the road and kept going.

Determined to get as far away as possible, the family didn't stop until they got all the way to Fort Concho in west Texas. They camped outside the fort, along with a few other families, until they found a small house just across the river in San Angelo.

Etta had become so afraid of white people, especially white men, she was afraid to go outside of their home.

If not for the black Buffalo Soldiers who were stationed at Fort Concho, Etta would never have met Daniel. His kindness to them, while they were camped near the old, nearly empty fort, eased her fears, but only enough to accept him, no others.

Daniel visited their home and family, repeatedly helping out and showing small kindnesses, finally gaining the courage to actually court Etta.

When she accepted his proposal of marriage, he almost couldn't believe his ears.

The Chaplin performed the ceremony in the little chapel at the fort. A small house just north of downtown San Angelo was their home for many years until they heard about sharecropping and decided to give farming a try.

Being a valiant Buffalo Soldier didn't necessarily equate to being a good farmer. A bad leg, poor soil, drought, no money, and sharecropper debt made it impossible to be successful at farming in the Hill Country. He retired from farming and helped out here and there for their neighbors.

After meeting a very nice lady named Sara Cain, Etta took a job at the Cain Hotel and General Store, where she quickly became known for her pies and homemade bread. For a long time, Daniel sat on the porch all day so Etta wouldn't be afraid. Fortunately, the kindness of her employer, and of most of the people who lived around there, began to help her to be less afraid and better able to let Daniel leave for the day. That was a very fortunate thing, as some of those kind folks had begun to complain about the black man sitting on the porch all day. Even in that warm and friendly place, it made some of the white folks uncomfortable about coming to the store or letting their children play near there.

Chapter Nine

Johanna paused on the bridge. "It seems like only yesterday that we crossed Sandy Creek for the first time, Father. We've been here over a month. This bridge looks the same as the one down by the encampment." But this bridge was different; it was on the part of Sandy Creek that belonged to the Terrell ranch. Sandy Creek and the Llano River both provided good fresh water for the many head of cattle that grazed there. The Pack Saddle Mountains, off in the distance, reminded Johanna of home, but unlike the colorful trees of the beautiful Blue Ridge Mountains back in Tennessee, they were covered in sagebrush and cedar and had a quiet beauty of their own. The similarity of the bridges resulted from the work of the Terrell ranch hands, always volunteering in efforts to move the country forward. Mike Terrell was a true, loyal, concerned Texan, a native son.

Mike grew up working the ranch with his father, who had been one of the successful settlers in the area.

Success had allowed him to buy ranches and farms that came available when others failed. Mike's only sibling had died shortly after birth. When his parents' long lives ended within days of each other, he was left with the ranch and no other family. The ranch was remote and many long hours were spent on the range or on a cattle drive. Mike had little opportunity to meet the right girl, so he'd never married. When he was younger, a cattle drive could last for months and would take him to the various forts in central and west Texas, Fort Concho, Fort Mason, Fort McKavett and others. The ranch had contracts with the cavalry back then, furnishing beef to the isolated forts. Some drives would take them away for even longer periods, herding cattle up north to Missouri or Kansas. The end of the drive meant a chance to visit a saloon and let loose a little or seek the comfort of a lady in the city. There was one particular lady in Abilene who he liked more than others, but she left Texas for a logging camp near Carson City and he never saw her again. Those days were past, though. Mike was too old for such foolishness, and now the drives were only the short distance to the cattle yards in Austin or San Antonio.

Most of the forts had long ago been decommissioned and abandoned and the government contracts along with them. Now the cattle were loaded onto trains and taken up north.

Mike seldom left the ranch anymore, but on occasion he would ride fence himself or sleep under the stars, holding on to old memories. On a hot night he still slept on a cot on the porch. The fall festival was one of the few events that got him off the ranch. The meetings of the Cattleman's Association were still important to him, but more frequently, he sent B.G. to take care of cattle business.

The Terrell Ranch was actively involved in eradicating Texas cattle fever. Mike had a fondness for the South Texas longhorns that often carried, but were immune to the ticks that carried it. They infected and nearly extinguished his imported cattle from England that had been brought over to breed with his longhorns. He was trying to produce a sturdy, heftier breed. Like other Texas ranchers, he had also been affected by the northern states' quarantines against Texas cattle. He tried taking his cattle to Colorado instead, but that didn't solve the problem. Gunfights with northern ranchers and cutting the fences erected to keep Texas cattle off their lands were no solution, either. He didn't want any more of his drovers, or himself, being shot.

Years earlier, on a Kansas City drive, one of his foremen hurriedly rode back to the ranch, arriving in the wee hours of the morning, sleepless and exhausted. His horse was lathered with sweat after being ridden hard for days. The herd had been confronted with barbed wire fence and gunmen, hired to prevent their entrance into Kansas.

Warning shots were fired into the air, and the conflict that followed involved gunfire between the drovers, the opposing ranchers and their hired guns. One of the drovers was grazed on the forehead by a bullet. Unable to move forward, the foreman hoisted a flag of truce and approached the fence and gunmen. He learned about the quarantine against Texas cattle and the suspicion that Texas cattle fever was caused by ticks. The ranchers up north were determined to keep those cattle and the suspected ticks away from their pastures. The foreman returned to the Terrell ranch. Mike joined him on his ride back to the herd to meet with the ranchers involved. The cattle were ultimately herded to west Texas to pasture for the winter. Mike became involved in the effort to keep peace with his northern brothers, and pledged to learn more about the tick problem.

Many years later, B.G. returned from a Cattlemen's Association meeting with news of a South Texas ranch that had begun dipping their cattle and were having success eliminating the ticks. The Terrell ranch quickly followed suit, setting up dipping operations, also. There had been some success, but dipping wasn't mandatory yet, so there was still work to be done. Many ranchers disagreed about the causes of the fever. Their longhorns weren't sick. They disagreed with the solutions, too. Holding their cattle in quarantine pastures for long periods of time or dipping a whole herd was costly and inconvenient.

Keeping the South Texas cattle or Mexican cattle restricted to the border area was an effort that would be difficult to enforce, as well.

Chapter Ten

One of the Mexican ranch hands was stationed at the gate. Johanna recognized him from the festival. His presence suggested that he was there to meet and escort them to the ranch house.

"Buenos Dios!"

The ranch house was not what Johanna expected. It was built of white limestone and huge cedar logs and posts. The porch that ran the length of the house, front and back, was adorned with a wrought iron fence with gates and sections fashioned in the shape of the Terrell ranch cattle brand. Set against the rustic old house, the decorative wrought iron looked out of place. It was plain to see that the welcoming, worn old house had served to enrich the lives of the Terrell's, their friends and extended family for many years.

B.G. was learning the business of the ranch and Mike's breeding programs. He was also conducting his own breeding program on a few acres of land that had been set aside for his use as a gift from Mike on his twenty-first birthday. Fenced off from the rest of the ranch, his new cattle didn't seem to be infected by the ticks. Hoping to develop bigger, heftier cattle that would adapt well to the Texas terrain was his goal. Success would mean a good start for his future and the money to buy his own place someday.

B.G. Steven was the grandson of Mike's father's best friend. That entire family was wiped out by typhoid fever when B.G. was a baby. That he didn't develop the illness was a mystery. Not knowing the whereabouts of any other family or relatives, Mike took him in. The ranch hands that worked for Mike and the ladies who cooked and kept his house helped raise B.G. He grew up on the back of a horse riding behind Mike or some other cowboy. B.G. was the son Mike would never have.

With the exception of the cattle that Mike gave to B.G., the rest of the cattle, the ranch and the entire Terrell estate would go to the university upon Mike's death. Mike had been his father's only heir and was the last of the Terrell family.

The last thing B.G. expected when he rode into town for the festival was to meet the prettiest girl he'd ever seen. She was a vision. He didn't want to leave her that night, and wanted to be with her again as soon as possible. He already knew that she had finished her schooling, knew she was working at the general store for Sara, and that her father would be coming to the ranch often. He was unable to hide his feelings and was hoping she felt the same.

Standing on the porch with Mike, B.G. was looking for only one rider. Two aroused his curiosity. He knew instantly the small frame was not a man. *Johanna!* As the distance closed between them he could see for certain that it was indeed Johanna. His heart rose in his throat as he and Mike stepped off the porch to greet their guests.

Lunch at the ranch included all the hands who were present, the family and any visitors who may have stopped by. The ranch hands, it appeared, did most of the cooking outdoors. Meat was cooked over open flames, but there were also large kettles and Dutch ovens resting in the coals where biscuits and pies were baked. Hanging over the fire on racks were frying pans sizzling with hot oil, filled with battered steak and chicken. A giant table was spread with vegetables and fresh bread. It was surrounded with enough unmatched chairs to seat the entire crowd. Mouths watering, they could hardly wait to eat. The ladies who lived and worked in the house greeted them in their broken English. It was a typical day at Terrell ranch.

Chapter Eleven

Over lunch Mike and Guenther realized how much they had in common: close in age, each raising a child, shared values. Both men were grateful for the twist of fate that had brought them together. When Guenther was planning to leave Tennessee, Mike had posted a petition at the telegraph office for a blacksmith in Texas. He was grateful to have found one. Guenther was grateful to have found a loyal customer, a friend, and a good place to call home.

After lunch, the two men made their way to the blacksmith shop located beside one of the barns on the ranch. Guenther was impressed at the equipment available there, an anvil, forge, bellows and all the tools typically used by a blacksmith or farrier. "Some of this has been here since long before my father died. We didn't always have a local blacksmith and did a lot of this work ourselves," Mike explained, as he brushed cobwebs away.

"When the blacksmith moved to the community and opened his shop, we began utilizing his skills, and later persuaded him to visit some of the area ranches," Mike went on. "There is enough work here and at the other ranches to make it worth the trip out here."

"What other ranches are interested in this agreement? Where are they located?" Guenther questioned Mike about the details. He knew being away from the shop too often could be a disadvantage to building the business. He hadn't met the other ranchers and there could be concerns about distance and payment.

Guenther had learned the hard way that even good people can't always be relied upon to pay. He left Tennessee with money owed to him. Money he knew would never be paid. He had even experienced hostility at times when trying to collect payment. He finally began demanding payment, or at least partial payment, before he started a job, especially a big job. He learned that the more indignant the reaction, the less likely he would be to receive payment. He had already decided that payment up front would be required at the shop. He had yet to make the decision about the ranches.

Mike and Guenther rode out to visit another rancher, leaving B.G. to entertain Johanna. Comfortable that the ladies in the house were present, they both left the ranch with no concern for their children.

"What luck!" Johanna and B.G. each thought to themselves, when Mike and Guenther rode away without them.

Other than a brief "Hello," neither of them had spoken a word since Johanna and Guenther dismounted. Mike had commented on the beauty and agility of Pebble, asking about the breed, as he had never seen such a horse. B.G. had said nothing until Mike and Guenther left.

"He is a beautiful horse. Where did he come from?" B.G. asked as he ran his hand down Pebble's long neck, patting him. Like Mike, he'd never seen the breed.

"Pebble was mother's surrey horse. My father accepted him as a guarantee for payment on a job he completed. My mother was so fond of him that my father agreed to let her keep him. She taught me how to ride on Pebble," she said, her voice quivering. Her mother's death still too recent, thoughts of her still brought Johanna to tears. "His breed is Andalusian. It is a Spanish breed."

B.G. would soon learn that Johanna was an accomplished rider.

"So, how is it that Mike and the people out here call you B.G.? What is your real name?" Johanna had wondered about it since they first met.

"B.G. is all I've ever known. My family died when I was young. The town we lived in burned to the ground, my birth records with it," B.G. explained.

B.G. asked Johanna about school. He was happy to learn that she had finished her education and had no further plans. She would not leave her father. He told her about his place and small herd and the breeding program going on at the ranch.

"We could ride out to my place and be back before Mike and your father return. Would you like to? I'd like for you to see it."

Johanna already had her boot in a stirrup, and shouted, "Lead the way!"

B.G. had done a lot of hard work on his place, and it showed. There was a small house with a covered porch set under large oak trees. He had planted several pecan trees and hauled barrels of water from the creek to keep those trees alive. He described how the digging of a well would be underway soon. A water douser had already found the spot for the well. The area was cleared and clean. Inside the house was a sleeping cot. One wall had cabinets and a sink stand. He nodded his head when Johanna asked, "Did you do this all yourself?"

Johanna stood in the middle of the room and admired B.G.'s handiwork. He came over and took her hand in his. Surprised, she turned to face him, but didn't pull her hand away. B.G. had never kissed anyone, but he pulled her into his arms. He hesitated briefly, then he kissed her. He held her face in his hands and first gently, then hungrily, kissed her. His legs almost buckled from desire. He kissed her mouth, her neck, her face and her mouth again. Johanna had only kissed one other person, Eli. That brief encounter seemed like a million years ago.

As much as she fondly remembered that first wonderful kiss, it did not compare to her feelings for B.G. Steven.

Johanna pushed him away. "We mustn't! What would you think of me? We must go! My father will be back and worried about me if we don't hurry!"

Pulling himself away, B.G. escorted her out of the house and helped her onto her horse. He stood for a moment looking up at her. "Johanna."

Johanna yanked the reins around, forcing her heels into Pebble's flanks. They raced back with the wind in their faces. Pebble forged ahead. B.G. watched Johanna expertly ride, gracefully gliding through the air as if flying above her horse.

Johanna was relieved that they arrived back at the ranch just ahead of her father. Guenther talked endlessly on their return trip to the hotel. Johanna heard little of his conversation. Her head was filled with her own thoughts about B.G. Steven.

᛭

B.G. gathered some gear and rode back to his house. He didn't usually stay out there, but this night he needed to be alone. He ate his dinner in the light of his lantern. He tried to read, but couldn't keep his thoughts straight. He finally gave up and went to bed. He would talk to Mike soon. He hoped for approval to speak with Guenther. Unable to sleep, there was no relief for the fire in his body that burned through the night.

Chapter Twelve

The numbers at the encampment continued to grow with people from the Hill Country, with migrants who had come West from eastern states and with immigrants who had packed up their homes in the old country and come in groups headed for Texas. Some were there temporarily, some had no place to go, and some were just travelers who stopped for the night. Reality sometimes met the new settlers at places like the encampment. They encountered families who had lost their farms and had abandoned failing settlements. They heard stories about those who had left for surviving settlements and towns and started over as merchants and tradesmen. They heard sad stories like that of a thriving community that lost most of its residents to typhoid fever, and the fire that destroyed the town.

Looking for a way to survive, some of the men at the encampment found work on a dam a few miles away, some at the granite or salt mine, and some learned of the cedar choppers who were earning money by chopping and selling cedar for posts or charcoal. The abundance of cedar throughout the countryside provided an opportunity for many of them to sustain their families. A day in the cedar break with an ax enabled them to scratch out a meager living. The demand for barbed wire fences by many of the ranchers afforded them the opportunity to chop and sell all of the cedar posts they could produce.

On his frequent trips to Austin to pick up supplies for the Cain's, Dodge Blackburn had become acquainted with many of the people at the encampment. He lingered for hours there and on occasion would stay overnight. He felt comfortable among those people, but other than his name, kept his identity and life to himself. A few structures had been built, a bathhouse and a privy outside the common area. Wagons, pulled close together with a canvas hung between them, made a large covered area. It created shelter from the sun and weather. Under it, children played and mothers struggled to make a home.

Out by the bathhouse there was a colorfully decorated wagon in which resided two attractive young ladies. Shunned by most of the other residents, their guests usually came and went at night. Their presence often created a ruckus. Mothers, trying to keep their teenage sons away, would come to chase the boys from the vicinity, shouting reprimands to the ladies. On occasion, a wayward or drunken husband was caught trying to sneak into their wagon. These two young ladies, Rosie and Cheri, moved from town to town, fort to fort, following soldiers, miners or railroad crews, appearing wherever a work camp sprang up. Their stay at the encampment would only last until the mine closed or the building of the dam was completed, or until the work crews moved on.

His heart empty, numbed by the past, lost in the present, Dodge would sometimes visit them. The pleasure of the ladies' company, and of liquor, if only for a few hours, could put the past out of his mind, and he could escape thoughts of Sara Cain in a place where no one else would know.

Few of the residents from the encampment ever visited the Cain General Store. More often they would travel in groups to Austin or other nearby towns. Many of the men rode into town looking for jobs, while others picked up supplies. Some would find day jobs and temporary work. There was always someone going or coming. Dodge often rode along with them.

Dodge had become friends with several men who also either lived there or frequented the encampment the same as he did. Also like him, they often stayed overnight. Two of them described themselves as cowhands from a ranch farther west. Another was a drummer who traveled all over the Hill Country plying his wares. The drummer would be the one most likely to stop by the Cain's store, and possibly recognize him some day. The encampment was a good place to lay over, in the safety of numbers.

The presence of strong determined men probably deterred any would-be robbers or troublemakers. Guard duty was shared by all of the able-bodied men. In spite of rumors and an occasional fight between the youngsters, there was seldom any trouble at the encampment.

Chapter Thirteen

Dodge rode in to Austin with his two cowhand friends that day. Once there, each went his separate way. Dodge visited an apothecary to pick up a specific tincture for Sara then stopped by their lawyer's office to drop off papers and pick up money. The three met up at Barton Creek Bridge for the trip back. Rather than stay at the encampment that night, the cowhands announced that they would be riding on out. Dodge decided to stay one more night in the colorfully decorated wagon.

⁎ⅎ

The encampment came alive in the middle of the night, when a sheriff's posse thundered into the clearing. A robbery had taken place that very day at a bank in Austin. Witnesses reported that two gunmen came into the bank and handed a note to the teller, while one waited outside holding the horses. They had escaped with several thousand dollars. No one had been harmed, but one customer followed the group to the outskirts of Austin, later stating that the outlaws had taken the road northwest toward old Fort Mason, which was the very road that crossed Sandy Creek near the encampment. The residents of the encampment recognized the men from the posse's descriptions, including Dodge. Everyone knew that Dodge rode out with the others the morning before. Efforts made in his defense were hopeless. No amount of explanation or protest could change the outcome. Dodge was arrested and transported to the jail in Austin.

He tried to still the panic rising from deep within him. It was reminiscent of the helplessness he felt as a small child when his mother handed him over to the agent on the train. It reminded him again how alone he felt after his adoptive mother died, and his adoptive father was taken away. He felt the desperation again when he was left at the orphanage in Galveston, wondering if he would ever have parents again, or if he should escape, which he had done.

Dodge paced the floor hour after hour, as day after day passed. He didn't want the Cain's to know about his arrest or that he had been visiting the encampment. Involvement there, and now this, could make him suspect in many questionable incidents and often false allegations against those people. That he had a secret life without their knowledge and had not returned with their money would create doubts about him. He knew the Cain's would have expected him to be back days earlier. His only hope was for the law to find or capture the outlaws soon. *Maybe, if they are found, I can be cleared as an accomplice to the robbery and released before any damage is done,* he tried to convince himself.

The saddlebags with the medicine and the Cain's money were hidden in the wagon that belonged to the ladies. Having no idea what lay ahead, he had hidden it as a precaution when he first arrived that evening. Had it been discovered, it might have been suspected as being the robbery money. It was not the safest place, but he could only hope that the ladies didn't find it and betray him.

The only thing anyone knew about those men was that they worked at a ranch farther west. People knew only their first names, Reed and Jackson. They had stayed overnight at the encampment a few times. Word was that they had committed other robberies. Dodge refused to believe it. He could only hope and wait.

A captain with the Texas Rangers out of Dallas, Dred Hill, had been put on the case. He took eyewitness accounts from the bank employees. He hadn't decided whether he believed Dodge Blackburn's story. The story was vague. Not wanting the Cain's to know what a mess he had gotten himself into, Dodge was withholding the very information that could probably clear him, specifically, the names of Sara and Abel Cain, who were barely a mile away from the encampment.

Several bank employees were brought to the jail to identify him, but they couldn't be certain he was the rider left outside to hold the horses. The man outside wore a tan western cowboy hat; Dodge wore an aged black slouch flat brim from England, given to him by Abel Cain many years ago. Easily recognizable, those hats were worn by the military. The gunman's hat was not a black slouch hat like the one Dodge wore.

Captain Hill still had to search for the two other men thought to be involved. *These three suspects might have just been in the wrong place at the wrong time, or at least Blackburn may have been. There could be another gang or a different member of the gang that met up with them at the bank and left by another route,* the captain reasoned. Arrangements were made for a deputy sheriff to accompany him to the encampment up at Sandy Creek.

Chapter Fourteen

Unpacking a new shipment at the general store, Johanna stood at a mirror admiring a new bolt of fabric. She had unwrapped it and was holding it across her chest. Her mother had been teaching her to sew, but her sewing machine was one of the items that had to be left behind. Sara caught a glimpse of her as she placed the fabric onto the shelf, and said, "Johanna, I have a sewing machine upstairs if you would like to use it. That piece would make a lovely dress."

Although Johanna had begun to prefer boy's trousers most of the time, a pretty dress was always nice for a special occasion. Sara Cain wore beautiful dresses made of linens and laces and other luxurious fabrics. Her usual choice of jeweled colors highlighted her raven hair and fair skin. Johanna knew Sara sewed many of her dresses, but sometimes ordered them through the catalog there in the store. Looking at the catalog was one of the things Johanna liked most about working there. Anything could be ordered, from houses to stockings. She referred to it as the *Dream Book*.

Johanna was busily stocking the shelves when she realized she was hearing Sara and Abel speaking in hushed tones. She heard them say Dodge Blackburn's name and could detect concern in their voices. She knew Dodge hadn't been seen in a week or so, and that he'd never returned from his last trip to Austin, which would have only taken a few days. Johanna knew he had gone for medical supplies for the store, but she did not know about the money.

Johanna heard them leave through the front door and watched as they crossed the street to the school. Luke Matthews met them at the door and stood speaking with them on the porch. She suspected they were talking about Dodge.

When the Cain's returned to the store Johanna boldly questioned them. "Has something happened to Dodge Blackburn?"

They shared their concerns about his wellbeing and their decision to wait one more day before starting out to look for him. He was always reliable, so their concern was that he had fallen victim to foul play or had an accident and was lying injured somewhere. "Luke Matthews is going out to search for him as far as the encampment at Sandy Creek at daylight. Maybe he'll find out something."

Guenther nodded and smiled as Johanna shared the events of the day, but the smile faded when she told him about Dodge Blackburn and about Luke's planned trip to the encampment. "Luke shouldn't go alone. I'll offer my help."

ഇൻരഃ

Luke and Guenther saddled their horses in the dim light of dawn. Uncertain of what the day might hold, they wanted an early start and hoped to return with good news.

Guenther hadn't been back to the encampment since their first and only night there. He wondered about some of the people he had met. Luke often stopped by there en route to another of his churches. On a few occasions he had held services. He worried about many of the people there. Some he had known from another settlement as church members whose farms had failed. He hoped good fortune had found them and that they were no longer forced to live at the encampment.

Their horses stepped into the rippling spring water of Sandy Creek. Guenther remembered Johanna's smiling face as she waded across when they were there before.

The encampment looked much the same. Luke was relieved that he didn't recognize any of the residents. The German family, with whom Guenther had spoken and shared coffee, was still there. They spoke again and Guenther explained the reason for their visit.

Chapter Fifteen

Henry Freeze sat at his table in the light of his lamp, pen in hand. With a heavy heart he prepared a note to send to his daughter. Days earlier, his wife Katherine had died suddenly.

Lured by the promises of success and wealth in America, Henry and Katherine had sailed from Germany together as young newlyweds. They crossed the Atlantic and landed in Galveston, Texas along with a ship full of fellow countrymen from their village. The port of Galveston received many immigrants.

Henry's family owned a haberdashery in Germany. Working in such a store was his profession. More fortunate than most, Henry's family had wealth, but he went to work on the docks and saved money until he and Katherine could manage to buy their general store without a loan.

Their precious Sara was born a few years later. Katherine had a difficult pregnancy and challenging birth, and as a result, they were not blessed with other children. They doted on their only child, teaching her to read and write before she even started school. Sara began to work in the family store helping her father and mother when she was just a toddler. By the time she was a teenager, she could manage the store as well as her parents.

The success with their store allowed the Freezes to invest in property in Galveston and carefully amass wealth. They created a sizable fortune. They funded Sara and Abel's store. Henry accompanied Sara and Abel and helped to establish their store before returning home to his own business.

He sent his close friend, Dodge Blackburn, to stay with and protect Sara, and to help her and Abel with the store. Henry was very fond of Dodge. Many years earlier he caught him sneaking into the store through an unlocked door, apparently to steal food and find warmth. He could see that the boy was in poor health. Something about the boy touched his heart. It had taken days to gain his trust enough that he would finally give his name. Rather than turn him over to the law, Henry decided to help him. He had never pressed Dodge about his past and had only learned small bits of information that slipped out on occasion.

Adopted off an orphan train in Kansas City as a small child, his new family moved to Galveston. His adoptive father was taken away after his adoptive mother mysteriously died. Discovered by authorities, he'd been placed in an orphanage but had escaped and survived on his own, still a youngster, pilfering garbage and sneaking food off grocery stands, until he ran into Henry Freeze.

Given the chance, Dodge had proved to be a good and loyal friend. Along with his own daughter, Sara, Henry had arranged for Dodge in his will. Although Dodge didn't know it, one day he would be a very wealthy man.

SARA...MOTHER DIED...
3:12 PM 11-21...REQUEST REPLY...

There were telephones in Galveston and in the Freeze General Store, but there were few telephones, if any, in remote areas of the state. So Henry made his way to the telegraph office, where a telegram could be transmitted to Sara. He knew Sara would come home, so he made no plans for a date to bury his sweet Katherine. He arranged for a burial vault and waited for word from Sara.

Sara's heart sank when she saw the Western Union rider stop in front of the hotel. A telegram usually meant bad news. Expecting to give directions to the rider, she was shocked that the telegram was intended for her. "Maybe it is news of Dodge," she exclaimed. The words on the telegram took her breath away. The rider helped her into the hotel, where Abel instantly ran to help her into a chair and read the telegram.

Fortunately, a train could take Sara the entire way to Galveston. The trip would take only a few days. She could catch a train at a depot nearby.

Without Dodge's presence, Abel couldn't leave the store or the guests at the hotel to accompany Sara. He would also need Johanna's help, so Sara had to go alone. Hopefully, Luke Matthews and Guenther would be back soon. One of them would need to escort Sara to the train station a few hours away.

Johanna cried with Sara and tried to offer comfort. Her own loss was still too fresh. She helped Sara pack her trunk for the trip. Not knowing how long Sara would have to be away, the trunk was packed full. There would be many things that needed to be done in Galveston.

Chapter Sixteen

It had been weeks since anyone from the Terrell ranch had been to the Cain General Store. They knew nothing of Dodge Blackburn's disappearance or Sara's mother's death.

B.G. had waited for the right opportunity to speak to Mike about asking for Johanna's hand. He was embarrassed and afraid he might have to take a ribbing from Mike, or worse, Mike might tell the other hands. He knew a ribbing would be coming from them for sure. He gathered the courage after dinner one afternoon, when Mike had settled himself on the porch in a comfortable chair.

When B.G. first approached Mike about Johanna, Mike was surprised. He wondered to himself how he had missed seeing the attraction between those two young people.

"How does she feel about…?" he questioned B.G.

"I'm pretty sure she feels the same way," B.G. replied.

Mike explained that Johanna was young, they had only seen each other a few times, and that Guenther would probably not give his approval.

B.G. began to defend his position, explaining his maturity, his success with his cattle, and the house he had already built and was enlarging. Mike finally agreed to join him on a visit to Guenther.

B.G. knew that Johanna cared for him. She hadn't said so, but he knew. It would take all the courage he could muster to talk to Guenther, and even more to propose to Johanna. More than anything, he feared her answer might be no.

His small house was originally only one room. If he was going to raise a family there, he knew he needed to add on to it, which he had begun the day after Johanna's visit. A chifferobe, for Johanna's clothing, and a four-poster bed were being built as a wedding gift. He had spent many hours putting nice carvings in the cedar and sanding it until it was as smooth as glass.

B.G. knew about her mother's china dishes, and planned to make a special cabinet for them, too. He had made many plans for their home, hoping she would accept his proposal. The use of that small piece of land, and being allowed to build that little house for his own use had been evidence of Mike's generosity. Building his small herd was a good start for their future.

B.G. had hoped that he and Mike could go see Guenther at the end of the week, but Mike reminded him about the Cattlemen's Association meeting, which would take him away from his desired plans.

Luckily, this time I only have to travel to San Antonio rather than some place farther away. I'll only have to be gone for a few days, but once I return, Mike and I will visit Guenther.

As B.G. left the ranch, he crossed Sandy Creek just outside the gate. He would cross it again, less than a mile away, at the bridge near the encampment. It had been a long time since he last passed through there. Johanna had told him about their night there and about what a sad place it seemed to her. B.G. had always passed it by and paid little attention to the people or their activities. He didn't know anyone there. He did know that they were suspected of stealing livestock from the nearby ranches and farms, although no one had been able to prove it. *One of these nights we'll catch 'em red-handed.*

As he crossed over the bridge, he met a wagon carrying two young ladies traveling alone in the opposite direction. Thinking that they looked like saloon girls, he wondered what they might be doing out in this part of the country. He nodded as they passed, and smiled about the cheerfully decorated wagon.

Texas Fever was still on the agenda at the association meetings. Fencing pastures, barbed wire, breeding programs and coexisting with sheep and goat ranchers were items on the agenda, as well. B.G. took careful notes for Mike, but his thoughts were not on the discussions.

Glad to finally be on his way, he planned to ride straight through, but soon found that a moonless night in unfamiliar territory was more difficult to traverse than he imagined. Fearful that his horse might stumble, he dismounted and built a small campfire for the night. A clearing on the bank of Cypress Creek offered a good place to bed down and water his horse. *Tomorrow will come soon enough,* he thought.

Chapter Seventeen

Dodge couldn't think clearly. The Ranger and deputy had gone up to the encampment at Sandy Creek. *Will they question the ladies? Did they find the saddlebags? Will he be able to uncover the answers needed to clear me? Have the cowhands from west Texas returned?* He continued to pace the floor and wait for answers.

Many years of experience had provided Texas Ranger Dred Hill with the ability to ask just the right questions and read between the lines. He could recognize a lie before it passed someone's lips. The people at the encampment, with whom he spoke, were forthcoming and honest with their answers. The residents who didn't approve of Dodge's visits to the ladies let that be known. Otherwise, they didn't think he would commit a crime. Unfortunately, none of them could offer an explanation for Dodge's activities in Austin on the day of the robbery, nor explain the whereabouts of the two cowhands. Also unfortunately, the ranger couldn't speak to the ladies. They were no longer there. Considering it a coincidence that they had left, and no doubt information from them would be unreliable, the ranger focused on other leads.

"Texas is a vast country." The ranger knew that finding those cowhands would be like finding a needle in a haystack. "If they are the criminals, they are probably long gone from all of Texas," he told the deputy.

He left instructions that if they returned to the encampment, assuming they weren't actual criminals, they should report to the Texas Ranger's office in Austin. "Their friend Dodge needs their help."

Jackson and Reed, no last names. Having so few leads made this case difficult. *Stopping at each sheriff's office throughout the area will be a start. I've had tough cases before. Besides, the bank is offering a reward for their capture. Wanted posters have been published and distributed. Someone must know something.* Fortunately for Dodge, no poster went out for him. He'd already been captured.

Dodge had been unwilling to furnish any personal information about where he lived or about any family connections. The ranger couldn't decide if it was because he was a criminal or if there was another explanation. He had one last question for the residents of the encampment. "Does anyone know where Dodge Blackburn comes from?" If anyone had ever known before, no one at the encampment now knew nor offered much of an answer to the ranger. Several stated they felt certain it was someplace close by, maybe a ranch or small town. They also said that sometimes he came in a wagon from Austin loaded with supplies.

Killings, bank robberies, horse thieving and cattle rustling were crimes that were not tolerated in Texas. This one robbery hadn't produced a big haul for the robbers, but if it were one of many, then they must be stopped. The ranger hadn't seen or heard clues to indicate there were more. Only a certain amount of time and manpower could be expended on this one crime.

This case reminded the ranger of a case a few years ago up in East Texas. There were many similarities. In that robbery two suspects went inside the bank while one other stayed outside with the horses. The witnesses to that robbery described the same men, as he recollected it. A trip to visit with the sheriff up there might be in order. *The time has come to put a stop to those old boys.*

Captain Dred Hill knew his next steps. He would continue his investigation in the local towns for a few days. He would let the wanted posters do the rest. "We'll see what the bounty hunters drag in. If something doesn't turn up soon, I've either got to charge Dodge Blackburn officially, or let him go."

Chapter Eighteen

Henry Freeze and Sara Freeze Cain embraced each other for so long that the train had begun to pull away again. They stepped onto a streetcar, which transported them to Tremont Street and the Freeze General Store.

There had been so much growth and change in the years since she had left Galveston that she hardly recognized the island city. Electric lights lined the city streets. Her father's store had a telephone.

A private service, with the priest and only the two of them, had been Katherine's request. Her vault was sealed in their presence and enclosed in an ornate white marble crypt, engraved with her name and the dates of her life and death.

VIĀRE

KATHERINE ROSE FREEZE

1836 – 1896

MT 16:24

Sara and her father talked into the night, sharing their memories. Henry relived their passage to America and talked about their life in Germany and the village in which they had lived and met. He told Sara about their decision to settle in Galveston rather than migrating further into Texas to the earlier land grants.

Sara again urged her father to sell his store and move to the Hill Country with her and Abel. "Soon, very soon," was always the answer.

While in Galveston, Sara seized on the opportunity to wander about the island. She wanted to stroll along the beach, smell the salty air of the Gulf of Mexico, and watch the gulls dipping into the water. She waded ankle deep, enjoying the waves as they splashed against her. She picked up a shell, and saw a tiny crab scurry sideways across the sand.

Not wanting to upset her father, Sara reluctantly told him about Dodge Blackburn's disappearance. She also told him about Dodge's trip to the attorney's office for money. She and Abel were very concerned, and although they'd searched, hadn't found him. Two of their friends had gone out to search for him. She described Luke Matthews, and went on to tell him about Guenther and Johanna Gurganis and their help in the search. Henry's concerns about Dodge's failure to come to Galveston and to Katherine's funeral were finally answered. He had hoped to see Dodge and had looked forward to his presence. Certain of Dodge's reliability, he assured Sara that Dodge and the money would return safely.

Before their visit ended, Sara had spoken about the events of the past eight years, those same events about which she had written many times. She missed talking with her mother, saddened by the reality that she could never talk to her again, nor look forward to the day her mother would join her in the Hill Country.

Not likely to return any time in the near future, she helped to sort through and pack away her mother's belongings.

Boarding the train and leaving her father behind, alone, was one of the hardest things she had ever done.

Sara had only traveled by wagon or stagecoach, and had never been on a train before this sad event, nor had she slept in a Pullman car. It had been nearly nine years since she had slept alone or hadn't had to hurry out of bed at dawn to start cooking breakfast. Overcome by lack of sleep, sorrow and exhaustion, she pulled the curtain on her berth. She lay looking out the window watching the glistening droplets from a light shower scatter like diamonds across the moonlit countryside. The rhythmic motion of the giant metal wheels lulled her to sleep. Peaceful sleep.

Chapter Nineteen

The visit to the encampment had sent Guenther and Luke back to the hotel with the information they all hoped to hear. Dodge Blackburn was alive and well. However, he had found himself in some trouble. The residents of the encampment shared the events of the past few weeks. Confident that Dodge would be released, they returned with their news, rather than going on to Austin. With Abel alone at the hotel and store, a trip to Austin would have to be postponed until Sara's return from Galveston.

Attending to the needs of the hotel guests had proven to be more work than Johanna realized. She and Abel were anxious for Sara's return. With Sara and Dodge both away, Abel became acutely aware of the burden they each carried.

Luke would meet Sara's train the next morning. Then he and Guenther would set out for Austin to secure Dodge's release.

Texas Ranger Dred Hill had been unable to find a sheriff anywhere who knew anything about or had ever heard of Dodge Blackburn. It appeared that he was a law-abiding citizen who happened to be in the wrong place at the wrong time. There had been no word from the cowhands, nor had the deputy turned up any information about them. The suspect had been held without being charged long enough. Dodge Blackburn would be released.

Knowing he was being released, and not charged with any crime, Dodge reluctantly provided the Ranger with a bit more information. Relieved that the Cain's had not been notified or questioned, he thought it unlikely the Ranger would ever visit the Cain Hotel and General Store.

Dodge walked out of the jail into the blinding afternoon sun, mounted his horse, Little Bit, and rode dead on for the encampment. He must get to the ladies as fast as his horse could carry him. He must retrieve the Cain's money.

Panic overcame him as he approached the encampment and could see that over near the bathhouse, where once sat the ladies' wagon, was an empty space.

Did they find the money? Dodge gasped. *Did they just move on to another work camp? Where did they go?*

He was met by warm greetings as he rode into the clearing. The residents were happy to see that he had been freed. They told Dodge about Luke and Guenther's visit, and that they had gone back to the hotel and general store to report the good news about his safety. Dodge wasn't happy to hear that they planned a trip to Austin to help with his release. It would be a long wasted trip only to discover that he was no longer there. He would be heading out to find the ladies and the Cain's money, and he wasn't going to hang around and let anything happen to prevent it.

Several days had passed since the ladies' departure. Word was they had set out for Oklahoma. Settlements and towns were springing up there. Settlers were still arriving from everywhere to take advantage of the remaining land, which had been made available by the passing of the Homestead Act, years earlier, and other later programs. Tenant farmers and sharecroppers were filling the state. When some failed, there were plenty of others to take their place. The expansion of the railroads brought many work crews. Opportunity abounded for Cheri and Rosie in Oklahoma.

Two ladies in a wagon would be traveling slowly. They'd be stopping in towns and old forts or settlements along the way, perhaps for several days at a time. On the Texas plains, much of it still Indian country, their safety would be at risk. He knew he could overtake them once he discovered their route. Until he was able to find them and retrieve the Cain's money, he would not rest or return.

Chapter Twenty

The dust from his arrival followed B.G. as he rushed through the doorway searching for Mike. He was anxious to share the speech he'd prepared for Guenther. It had been carefully rehearsed in his head for the past week or so. He didn't want to waste any more time waiting for the opportunity to fulfill his dream and take the biggest step of his life. Undaunted by Mike's laughter, the words continued to spill forth.

"First things first," Mike insisted on reviewing the notes from the Cattleman's Association meeting, along with any other pertinent information B.G. could remember. It was clear that his attention had been elsewhere. There was one good piece of information that B.G. did not forget. "Laws are going to be passed to make dipping mandatory," B.G. explained. "Finally, Texas Cattle Fever can be controlled or eradicated."

Mike had one of the hands hitch the wagon. As long as he was going toward the general store, he would pick up the supplies he had ordered. Lately, he'd decided the wagon was a bit more comfortable than straddling a horse. Now, it was B.G. who was laughing, as he watched Mike set his backside on a cushion.

Predictably, they found Guenther standing over his anvil, pounding out a wagon wheel. Sweat beaded on his hot forehead. His red face lit up with a broad smile, as he recognized his visitors. He greeted them in his usual jovial manner, "My good friends. Come in!"

While B.G. worked up the courage to make his speech, Guenther and Mike caught up on local events and gossip. It was the first they had heard of Dodge Blackburn's dilemma. At that moment, no one had heard the news that Dodge wouldn't be returning. Dodge was a vital part of the community. His absence was significant. So very fond of Sara, they were both saddened to hear of her absence and about her mother's death. "I'm going to drop by over there to pick up some supplies. I'll give my condolences to Abel. This is bad news for them, both Dodge Blackburn and Sara's mother. I hate hearing this," Mike said, as he turned to look at B.G., nodding to him to get on with his speech.

B.G. cleared his throat and Guenther looked up at the young man. "May I have a word with you, Mr. Gurganis?"

Guenther removed his apron and gave his full attention to the nervous young man.

The surprise of his life came to B.G. when he received no resistance to his request for Johanna's hand. He suspected that Guenther had not overlooked the obvious attraction they shared for each other. Perhaps his rehearsals had paid off. Although it seemed unnecessary to make his entire speech, his persistence provided Mike and Guenther with a good amount of entertainment.

Guenther Gurganis was a very wise man. His opinion of B.G. was favorable. He knew Johanna would hope for his approval of her marriage and her choice of a husband. He remembered that morning, not too long ago, when he and Johanna rode out to the Terrell Ranch, when he suddenly realized that his baby girl had become a woman. He also remembered that he and Elizabeth had married late in life and wished that he could have spent his whole life with her. If he opposed, there would be no end to it. Guenther also realized that the selection of worthy young men in their area was lacking. Eligible young men were few and far between. She may not have another good opportunity like B.G. Steven. The decision would be hers, with his blessing. Besides, he was getting up in years, he was happy to start thinking about grandchildren.

Chapter Twenty-one

Luke Matthews was always helpful in any situation, but he truly wasn't looking forward to seeing Sara. Her sad, tired face made him wish he could help, but he knew there wasn't really anything he could do, other than to pray with her. It had been a terrible shock to receive that telegram and learn of her mother's death. The trip, no doubt, would be tiring and difficult. Having to go alone, equally difficult. He knew how much Sara wanted her parents to come live with her and Abel. Luke was close to both of them. They'd shared their concerns and worries and joys with him, and their disappointment about having no children. Sara had given up hope. Knowing she would be feeling even worse right now, he dreaded her arrival. Hopefully, the good news about Dodge would lift her spirits. He continued looking down the tracks, waiting for a glimpse of the Katy train in the distance.

"Has there been any word about Dodge?" Luke was surprised that Sara's first words were to express her concern for Dodge. His report brought a smile. "Thank God he is safe!" Relief spread across Sara's face. As they rode along, he filled her in on the details, all the while observing that she seemed much more refreshed than he'd expected.

Sara had another request for Luke. "When everything settles down, I need to visit our lawyer in Austin on my father's behalf. I would appreciate it if you could accompany me."

The hotel, general store, and café would be back to normal, finally. Sara was back. Johanna and Abel had pledged themselves to be more help than before. Her absence had made them realize the amount of her work.

The next morning Luke and Guenther got an early start for Austin and the Sheriff's Office. "Dodge is going to be surprised to see us." Their happy banter continued for the duration of their trip.

The discovery that Dodge had been released several days earlier sent Luke and Guenther on a hurried trip back to Sandy Creek and the encampment. The residents had quickly extinguished any hope that he was there or that he might have returned to the hotel, when the explanation was made about the ladies leaving for Oklahoma. Although not knowing why, the residents suspected that Dodge left to pursue them. There was nothing left for Guenther and Luke to do, but return to Sara and Abel with this unfortunate, strange news.

They tried to think of a gentle way to report it to Sara. They dreaded being the bearer of more bad news. That Dodge was safe might still be a comfort, but this big puzzle and his failure to return would surely be another disappointment.

Only Sara and Abel Cain and Henry Freeze knew that Dodge was transporting money when he disappeared. They were unconcerned about the money itself, but rather for the dangerous situation it might create. They were confident about his decision to pursue the ladies; certain there was a good reason and a deliberate plan. Their only concern was for Dodge, that he return safe and sound and soon.

"He is safe, Sara, and he will come back. You must have faith," Luke assured her.

�✻ഇ

Always there when needed, everyone had learned to depend on Luke. But there was really very little known about Luke Matthews. In the years they all knew him, even from the very beginning, when he showed up to claim his uncle's small farm, his service and kindness had been accepted without question. No one ever asked about his life; they never thought to ask. He went about his quiet ways, tending to the school children, weddings and funerals.

No one knew about the blue-eyed beauty with black silky hair and fair skin, his betrothed, for whom he waited. Her family was coming west to Texas from Georgia. They had met at a church picnic in Atlanta, when he had just finished seminary. They corresponded back and forth for years. Each letter expressed her love and eagerness to join him, hinting at the wonderful wedding they would have and the life together that lay ahead.

Luke went about the business of taking care of his church and the members. He gained several churches as time passed and as his fellow preachers retired or moved to other areas. The churches kept him busy, but he also devoted his time and effort to help build a barn, a home, a school or a church.

His most joyful times were at the fall or spring festivals in the little community by Sandy Creek, near to his farm. Those folks knew how to have a festival. Sara and Abel Cain and Mike Terrell and all the rest knew how to do it.

Becoming dear friends with many of those people helped to fill the empty space in his heart that waited for Molly Oglethorpe. He was often invited for Sunday dinners, and he especially enjoyed the food when a barn or house was going up and all the ladies brought special dishes. There was a sad side to becoming friends with all of them. When they had troubles or lost a loved one, it was hard to lose those friends, too, and hard to see their pain.

He made a little money from his farm, and that was a good thing. Not many folks out in the country had extra money to pay a preacher.

He worked on his little farmhouse. He painted all the rooms and had put some curtains in the windows. It wasn't much, but it would be a good start for a young couple. He wrote to tell Molly about every project. Each of her letters expressed her delight and eagerness to join him.

Luke's father was a preacher in South Carolina. That was where Luke was born. All of his family was still there. Having an adventuresome spirit, he had joined the next wagon train when he heard about his uncle's farm in Texas. He was filling a temporary position at the church in Atlanta when he met Molly. A permanent job, out in the wild west, had sounded exciting.

Luke began to realize that Molly's letters had become slower to come. The responses became short, and the tone changed from sweet and anxious to cool and reluctant. Then they just quit coming. He wrote several more letters begging for a response, at least an explanation, but none ever came. Luke was heartbroken, certain that Molly had accepted another beau. He wanted to share his burden and sadness with someone, but he couldn't. No one had even known Molly existed, and more than that, he was supposed to be a source of comfort and strength, and draw his own comfort and strength from his Creator.

So, Luke went about his quiet ways.

Chapter Twenty-two

Just across the river from Fort Concho were saloons and gambling, dance halls and brothels. Unpopular with the upstanding citizens of San Angelo, it was popular with soldiers, cowboys and buffalo hunters. The doorway to vast, isolated west Texas, the city drew them like an oasis.

If Rosie and Cheri were ever going to get to Oklahoma, it was time for them to move on. Confident about their travels so far, they had no reservations about setting out for Oklahoma.

San Angelo had been a boon for them. They had earned enough money to sustain themselves until they arrived at Fort Sill. They would have the luxury of not working for a while unless they chose to do so. Some of the cowboys, with whom they'd become acquainted, directed them to Abilene and on up through Wichita Falls. The Oklahoma border was just the other side, and the next stop would be Fort Sill.

Rosie and Cheri, daughters of prostitutes, and friends since childhood, hoped for the same things. The circumstances of their birth and life didn't keep them from having the same hopes and dreams as any other young woman.

Along with the rapid growth of Oklahoma, the vastness and rapid settlement of the West brought men from everywhere. The lack of available women sometimes opened up opportunities for girls like them to find husbands.

෨෬

Maw'wat and his band of renegades took their time riding back to camp. Their raids throughout west Texas had been very successful. There were, no doubt, Federal troops searching for them, but so far, they'd been able to outsmart them and stay a few days ahead.

It was time to move the camp. Across the plateau along Johnson's Creek below the Llano Estacado, had been a good place to avoid discovery. The bluffs and canyons provided good shelter. They couldn't go farther north. There was too little water up on the mesa. If they weren't careful, they'd run into cowboys on some of the big ranches that had sprung up on the public lands.

Often encountering miles and miles of barbed wire fence, Maw'wat would be further enraged at the white man's destruction of the land. The life that his forefathers knew no longer existed. It didn't take ranchers long to gather a posse. *It is time to move on, before our camp is discovered,* he sneered.

The son of an Indian Chief, Maw'wat's father had been shot and killed when resisting life on a reservation. Forced from their homes and lands in Texas before he was born, Maw'wat spent his whole life moving from one camp to another, staying out of sight, avoiding Federal troops. He was guilty of many crimes, but blamed for many more. Now, hardened and heartless and filled with rage, he and his dwindling band sustained themselves the only way they knew, pillaging. If they had to, they killed anyone who got in the way. Maw'wat knew that it would be only a matter of time until the troops caught up with them. *It might be time to move on across the Mexican border or to No Man's Land up north. We'll make one last raid before we leave, and it will have be a good one,* he thought. Their marauding had produced a lot of bounty, but now they needed enough to last a long time.

With bellies full of mescal, Maw'wat and his renegades were braver than usual. They had ventured farther than they had set out to, but it looked as if they'd come upon a prize.

Holding his plundered nautical spyglass with his only good hand, he could see a brightly decorated wagon adorned with ribbons and ruffles. Set among the wildflowers, it was a sight to see. It brought him one of the few out-loud laughs his band had ever heard. The smile remained, but his lips slowly curled down at the corners. The wagon was carrying two women. From that distance, it appeared they were alone.

The landscape had flattened. The mesquite trees had begun to disappear. Acres and acres of golden grasses speckled with purple and orange and yellow wildflowers swept across the flatland. An abundance of colorful butter-flies and bees busily went about their business of visiting each flower. Rosie and Cheri sang songs and chatted as they crossed the prairie. Their voices blended with those of the thousands of prairie dogs, chattering among them-selves, their burrows scattered through the grass for pro-tection. They could scurry in quickly for safety. The prairie dogs could sense danger when it was imminent.

Chapter Twenty-three

Sara immersed herself in a welcome distraction: sewing Johanna's wedding dress. She had ordered the elegant white fabric a long time ago and kept it wrapped and stored away. She knew the day would come when someone in the community would need it. Otherwise, it might take months to wait for its arrival. Working in her father's store in Galveston, and living life in the Hill Country for nearly ten years had taught her a lot about planning ahead.

The news of B.G. Steven's proposal to Johanna Gurganis had traveled fast throughout the community and countryside. One thing about it, all of the residents who lived there and in the surrounding area were like one big family, and everyone knew everything about each other. There was some comfort in that, but Sara was tired of answering questions about Dodge Blackburn. Although grateful, she was also tired of politely receiving condolences and so frequently being reminded about her mother. Her trip to Galveston on a train and sleeping in a Pullman car was an endless topic for discussion. Every new encounter brought the same questions. Of course, there wasn't a lot in the community to talk about, so all of the recent activity had created a good bit of interest and excitement. *At least the wedding announcement might finally take some of the attention away from me,* Sara sighed.

The fact remained that she was still very upset about the loss of her mother. She was consumed with despair. She had not only lost her mother, but also a big part of her own future. Her parents would never join her in the Hill Country, one of the few things that had sustained her. She couldn't look forward to the day when she and her mother would be together again. Her mother would not be there to help with the delivery of her baby, if she were ever to become pregnant. Her children would not have a grandmother. They had always enjoyed each other's company, sharing and doing things together, like sewing Johanna's dress. Without her mother present to encourage her father, he would never leave the familiarity of their home. *He will never leave mother, now.* He had already made it clear that he wanted to be buried beside her. He'd even made arrangements for himself for when it was his time. Although he assured Sara that he would join them soon, she knew it would never happen.

The answers to questions about Dodge were equally difficult. His behavior was as big a puzzle to her as to anyone. Sara's thoughts rambled. *He doesn't even know about Mother. Why is he following those ladies to Oklahoma, if indeed that is where he went? Why would he just up and leave us? Maybe he has decided that he does want a life for himself. He has spent plenty of years working and doing for us. At least he is safe. Surely, we will hear from him soon.* Her concerns about Dodge and the feeling of loss, was a bit of a surprise to her. He had always been present, always attentive, taken for granted, maybe. Her feelings were conflicted and confusing. *At least I still have Etta.*

୨୦୧୫

Johanna and Sara had put their heads together, looked through the *Dream Book,* and found beautiful dresses. Sara knew how to make a pattern, and by combining several patterns that she already had, they had created an exquisite dress, just like the pictures in the catalog. Sara sewed the dress. With some helpful instruction, Johanna stitched on the lace and worked on her veil, taking particular care that it was perfect. They decided to layer the bodice of the dress with some of the same lace fabric that made up the veil. Johanna wanted to make the veil by herself, something special to keep forever.

There were many things in Johanna's hope chest that had to be left behind when they made their journey West. The special items that her mother had made or saved for her were burned when her belongings had to be destroyed. The only thing Johanna could proudly take to her marriage was her mother's china, which had been passed down through the family for many, many years.

From her own wedding, Sara still had her undergarments, petticoats and beautiful white lace-up shoes that, luckily, fit Johanna. Johanna's trousseau was complete.

Sara knew that without her mother, Johanna needed help with her wedding and plans. She wanted to be there for her. Sara decided she would encourage Johanna's questions about marriage and the responsibilities she would face as a wife. She remembered making her own wedding plans with her mother.

She hadn't taken the time to let her father know she had returned home safely, that her trip was uneventful, actually restful. She also needed to let him know that arrangements had been made to visit their lawyer and to deliver the important papers with which she had been entrusted. And finally, that Dodge was safe, but still had not returned. She doubted that Dodge's continued absence would influence her father's arrangements. If Dodge never came back, she knew her father's plan would stay the same.

"I'll pen a letter tonight," Sara concluded.

Chapter Twenty-four

Dodge decided the best plan to locate the ladies would be to travel from fort to fort. There were few places where the ladies would be welcome to spend a night or two. Even though the forts were mostly abandoned, there were often small settlements that had sprung up around them, and were still occupied by ex-soldiers or cowboys. Two nights, here and there, would allow him to close the gap between them. *It should close the gap between the recovery of the Cain's money and me, too.* He didn't want to think about the possibility the money could be gone. He would never be able to face the Cain's again. Allowing his horse to rest a bit, and drink from one of the many creeks or springs along the way, would be the only reason he would stop. He even bought fodder at a farm store near Fort Mason, so he wouldn't have to stop for more than a few minutes to feed his horse. He made one last stop near old Fort McKavett to look for signs the ladies had been there. It didn't appear they had, and there wasn't anyone who could confirm it.

They must not be resting as much as I'd suspected. He recognized the need to quicken his pace. *It will take all day to get to Fort Concho,* he reasoned.

Dodge found there was little or no activity at Fort Concho. Like the many other forts throughout Texas, it was virtually abandoned. He found saloons and the availability of prostitutes along the little street just across the river. *Maybe I'll find the ladies here.* Dodge went from place to place. He began asking bartenders and cowboys if they'd seen two young ladies together. "They live in a wagon together and they might be talking about going to Oklahoma." Finally, one bartender recognized their description. "They were only here for a few days. I guess they've left, because I haven't seen them today."

Dodge wanted to go on, but sleep was overtaking him. He hadn't laid his head down since the last night at the jail. He had to rest. It was late and dark, so he checked into one of the hotels. At least, now certain of the time they left and direction they had taken, they couldn't be more than a day or so ahead.

Awakened by the sun shining on his face, he jumped up, pulling his pants and boots on quickly. He hurried downstairs and confirmed his directions to Oklahoma. His map was not the best, and he'd never been in west Texas. It was totally unfamiliar territory. He replenished his supplies before heading out, not knowing when there'd be another opportunity. He had the same instructions as the ladies: Abilene, Wichita Falls and Fort Sill. It would take at least three long days to get to Fort Sill. He was confident he could overtake the ladies before then.

Feeling more anxious each mile, Dodge stayed on course, but he couldn't keep his thoughts from drifting back over the years that he had spent with the Cain's and the Freezes. Henry and Katherine Freeze were the best people in the world. *Sara, lovely Sara, you will never be mine.* He began to imagine that the money might never be recovered, a thought that he hadn't allowed to enter his head up until now.

He had hoped to catch up with the ladies long before now, but he knew, or at least hoped he knew, that they were going to Fort Sill. "If not before, I will find them there," he said out loud.

Up ahead, but still a good distance away, Dodge could see the smoke from a campfire. His heart leapt, as he hastened Little Bit's gait. "It's them!"

He quickly realized that it was much more than a campfire. As he approached, he could see it was a grass fire, and it was moving swiftly across the prairie. The wind was blowing the smoke and the flames toward him. He took off in the opposite direction, making a wide circle around the fire. Once he'd discovered that he had passed the origination point, he began to circle back. The fire had created its own storm. Smoke and soot and ash filled the air and darkened the once clear blue sky, blocking out the sun.

He came upon the metal frame of a wagon. Beneath it were the remains of the wagon itself, collapsed into a smoldering pile of glowing hot rubble. There was no sign of the horses. There was no sign of the occupants. Clinging to the charred remains of a sunflower stem was a slightly blackened pink ribbon fluttering in the relentless winds blowing off the plains.

A layer of soot and ash covered the prairie. Breathing was difficult. Even though Dodge had escaped the fire, his clothes and horse were covered with soot and ash. Finding hoof or footprints was almost impossible. The wagon was burned beyond recognition, but he knew it was Rosie and Cheri's wagon. For him, the pink ribbon was proof enough.

He stirred through the hot remains, searching for the saddlebags, still hoping for some small glimpse of leather. There was nothing. The saddlebags were gone and the money with them. He thought it unlikely that the ladies had ever found it. No doubt, the renegades took it and anything else of value. He sat in his saddle, frozen, allowing the events of the past few months and the devastation around him to sink in.

His thoughts turned to the ladies. He was certain they had encountered Indian renegades. The fact that they or their bodies weren't there told him they'd been taken.

Vomit suddenly spewed from his mouth. Knowing what they would endure made him sick. He knew they would be tortured and worse. *I have to try to save them! Maybe it won't be too late. These remains are still hot. They can't be very far ahead.* Dodge was relieved his supplies had been replenished when he left San Angelo.

"Little Bit, let's go find the ladies."

Dodge turned his gaze toward the West. Surely they would still be within sight, but the sun was creating a blinding reflection. He couldn't see beyond it. The prairie grass thinned in that direction. He hoped he could find and follow their trail. Although it was a very long distance, the border was in that direction. *They're headed for the border. I'm sure of it.*

Any hope of ever finding the saddlebags and the money was finally gone. "Any hope of returning to the Cain Hotel and General Store, to the Cain's, or to the Freezes, is also gone," he admitted to himself.

Dodge pulled on his black slouch hat, tipping the brim down in front to block the glare. He took a silent inventory as he did so. He had a Winchester rifle and a Colt Peacemaker, plenty of ammunition for both, a Bowie knife and a rope. More powerful than guns and ammunition, was a man who had nothing to lose.

What he would do, if he actually caught up with them, hadn't really crossed his mind. He would have to figure that out as he rode into the west Texas sunset.

Chapter Twenty-five

B.G. worked tirelessly on his place. Inside and out, it had to be perfect. He had spent every extra minute he could spare finishing the house, the furniture, and getting it all clean. The only thing he hadn't completed was an indoor washroom, which would be the next undertaking. He didn't want Johanna to have to haul water from the well and figured if a pump could get water to the house, it could get water inside the house.

He looked forward to the day electricity would be available to the Hill Country. He had read about it, and Sara Cain had told everyone about the electricity in Galveston. All of her stories about Galveston made him wish for a day when he and Johanna might visit there. *Maybe we could go there for a honeymoon someday.* He had never seen the ocean. His trips had been only cattle drives and a few errands for Mike to Austin or San Antonio for the Cattleman's Association meetings.

The cattle drive that was coming up in the fall would be the longest drive on which B.G. had ever been. The cattle were going to a ranch in Nebraska, and that rancher didn't want to bother with rail, as it was sketchy through parts of west Texas and Oklahoma. Mike was selling most of his new crossbred cattle that were the result of his longhorn mix with the English imports. It was an exciting time. There were no long drives like that anymore. Some of the older hands were looking forward to it. If Mike were a little younger, B.G. knew he would be going along, too. *Just like the old days*, he thought.

Landowner issues had to be dealt with. Sometimes they were accommodating and sometimes they would forbid anyone to cross their land, or would charge an arm and a leg for passage. The Indians allowed peaceful passage through their territory, usually for little more than a few beeves a day. This long drive would take a lot longer than drives used to take. Even in the old days and under the best circumstances, a herd moved only ten to twelve miles a day.

The difficulty of the upcoming cattle drive was the reason B.G. wanted to get married beforehand. *I have already waited long enough,* he lamented. There was no way to know how long he would have to be gone on the drive. The hands had talked about drives lasting many months. Even though they were looking forward to it, they were also grumbling about how long this one was probably going to take. He couldn't wait that long to hold Johanna in his arms and make her his wife. His heart took an extra beat every time he thought about it.

Especially proud of having ordered bedding from the general store, he'd ordered a coverlet, also. Sara Cain had kept it a secret. Johanna would be surprised to discover such fine linens on their bed. She had been working on a wedding ring quilt that would be finished by winter. It would be a surprise, and beautiful, for sure.

The pecan trees were doing well. Hauling water to them since the day they were planted had required determination. Once their taproot was deep enough they would survive. A good rain hadn't fallen on the Hill Country in a long time. Everyone was beginning to be concerned. Many gardens were drying up.

He had spent a lot of time clearing away the rocks out back to make a good space for a garden. He'd planted only a few things, but without rain, nothing was doing well. At least the deer were enjoying the melons.

Mike had his ranch hands lay pipes from the creek to irrigate some of his garden. It worked well, but would only reach the lower part of the garden. All the fruit trees were doing okay, so they would at least have canned peaches and apricots for winter.

Without rain, the weather was hotter than usual. It was pretty uncomfortable in the heat of the day and difficult to sleep at night. "A good rain would sure help," he said.

♊♃

B.G. and Johanna's wedding was just a few weeks away. They would have only a brief time together before he would have to leave on the cattle drive. They had been to see Luke Matthews to discuss the ceremony and make sure they knew what to expect. Some of Luke's conversation was embarrassing. It made Johanna blush and made B.G.'s heart take an extra beat again.

Sara Cain was going to be Johanna's matron of honor. Mike was going to be B.G.'s best man. Mike was indeed B.G.'s best man, the best man in the world. "I owe everything to him. If not for Mike, I would have ended up in a children's home. There is no way to know what would have become of me," B.G. said.

Although he knew it was deserted, he occasionally thought about riding over to the little town where he was born. He was told that a fire had destroyed the whole town, but not before almost everyone had died from typhoid, including his family. He was too young at the time to re-member it.

There is probably nothing there to see, maybe some old buildings, but the cemetery is still there. It might be nice to look for family names, B.G. thought. He had never gone back, but something about his upcoming wedding made him lonely for family.

Chapter Twenty-six

Dodge thought he was having hallucinations. He was certain he was looking at peach trees. *Are those peach trees in the middle of a desert?* He wanted to see up close, but had to hang back. He didn't dare risk showing himself.

He knew he wasn't far behind the Indian renegades. Surely they knew he was tracking them. Hardly stopping at all, they hadn't built a fire, either because of him or suspicious there were Federal troops in the area. "That sure would be a blessing!" Dodge said out loud. "What I would give for someone who could help." Cautiously staying low, he was sure the Indians would send a lookout to find who was behind them. He knew that one lone man, himself, could be easily captured. *Maybe there's someone else out here somewhere, someone they can see, but I can't see.*

Dodge could faintly smell smoke, but he didn't know where it was coming from. *It smells like food cooking, but what, or who? Is it other Indians? This isn't hospitable territory. I wonder if they are friend or foe?*

One thing gave him some comfort. The renegades hadn't been able to stop long enough to harm the ladies, if they hadn't already. There had been no evidence of it along the way.

He was grateful for the sleep he had at the hotel, because he couldn't risk sleeping now. He rummaged through his saddlebags for some jerky. It would have to hold him until he could shoot a rabbit and build a fire himself. A small sip of water from his canteen would have to do. He didn't know when there would be an opportunity to fill it again.

There weren't many places to conceal Little Bit or himself, but some sagebrush here or there offered a little shelter, not much. Finally, tying Little Bit securely to a mesquite, he moved forward alone. Each move put him more at risk, but he stayed at it.

Dodge wondered if the ladies knew there was someone on their trail, someone who knew that they were captives of Indian renegades, someone there to help them. He didn't really know for certain if the ladies were with the renegades or if they were still alive, for that matter.

There was a ridge between him and where he suspected the renegades had stopped to rest. If he could make it to the ridge, maybe he could determine how many of them there were, and whether the ladies were definitely with them. Waiting until after sunset only meant they would have more time to get liquored up and turn their attention to the ladies. He had to risk it.

He ran, darting from one scant bit of shelter to another, leaping into a gully just under the edge of the ridge. He had no idea what he would find. Thankfully, a hard landing was the worst of it. He checked himself over for scratches and broken bones, but there were none. Best of all, he had made it to the gully undetected.

He could actually hear them talking. It sounded like one of them was yelling at the ladies, but Dodge couldn't understand what was being said. They were all laughing and hollering, but their tone was not a happy one; it was rather menacing instead. Then he was shocked to hear what sounded like Rosie, cry out, "No, no!" He heard screams that sounded like both of the ladies, and he knew without a doubt they were there.

"It has to be now!" Dodge jumped out of the gully and ran as fast as he could, with every bit of strength he had, holding his Colt in one hand and his Winchester in the other.

Cherie was leaning against a large boulder. There were four renegades pulling Rosie in every direction. Her clothing was torn and tattered. She was mostly naked, making no sound, offering no resistance. It appeared she had fainted. One of the renegades sat on a rock, away from the frenzy, watching and smiling. He had the smile of a devil. He was looking back and forth, from Cherie to the scuffle that was occurring around Rosie's lifeless form. Cherie's shiny blond hair had saved her. Maw'Wat was keeping her for himself.

Dodge knew his first shot had to be his best, the most efficient. He had to determine the leader quickly and shoot him first. It was clear to him that the leader was the devil sitting on that rock, while the others had their way with Rosie.

What seemed like hours took only seconds. One carefully aimed shot hit Maw'Wat in the head. The second shot hit the Indian renegade who was raping an unconscious Rosie. Surprise and mescal had been Dodge's ally. The other three stumbled drunkenly to their horses. He didn't waste his effort on trying to stop them, but fired several more shots for good measure, possibly hitting one as they rode away.

He was more concerned about Rosie. Cherie fell to the ground, sobbing, while Dodge ran to Rosie. Pushing the dead renegade off her, he felt for her pulse. It was so faint, he was certain she wouldn't make it.

Suddenly, from behind, there was a loud commotion, yelling and gunfire. He turned and raised his gun to shoot, but lo and behold, there stood Reed and Jackson, his old cowhand friends from the encampment, the other two falsely accused bank robbers. They were too late to help, but a sight for sore eyes, just the same. They'd heard gunfire, recognized Little Bit, and came running.

Dodge turned back to Rosie. With their help, and talking fast, he described the events of the recent past, culminating in the scene that lay before them. Reed and Jackson knew the ladies. They had paid their visits to the pink ruffled wagon themselves. Lifting Rosie gently, carrying her to a shaded spot, they covered her and wiped her face with moistened rags, using the last of the water in the canteen. There was blood in her hair where she must have fallen on a rock. Rosie's pulse became more and more faint as each minute passed. There was no way they could move her, no place to take her, not likely she could be saved if there was someplace to take her.

There was no one to be notified of Rosie's death. Her only family was Cheri. They buried Rosie out in the west Texas desert, near San Solomon Springs, where cool clear water rushed forth from deep within the earth.

Reed and Jackson explained their presence in that part of the state. They worked on a ranch in New Mexico and came by there so they could stop at the springs for water.

Those were peach trees Dodge saw that night. He wasn't having hallucinations, after all. Hidden from his view the evening before, was a small settlement just on the other side of the ridge. The local residents irrigated their trees and crops through trenches dug from those springs.

The Mescalero Apaches did the very same thing, many, many years before the white settlers ever came to Texas.

Chapter Twenty-seven

"First my wife and now my daughter to marriage," Guenther muttered. After the marriage proposal Guenther was relieved that he hadn't purchased that house and piece of land he'd viewed with Mr. Fields. Johanna would be leaving to live with B.G. after the wedding. A whole house for him, alone, was unnecessary. He was not prepared to be alone, but could not deny his daughter her happiness.

The rooms above the shop would be plenty of space for him. He could cook anything he wanted right there in the shop and bathe under the pump out back. Besides, he had been taking most of his meals at the hotel cafe and may as well continue to enjoy Sara and Etta's good food. *Yes sir, I have saved myself a lot of work and money by dragging my feet on that decision.*

Blacksmithing was hard, hot work from which Guenther hoped to retire soon. Now that Johanna would be married and in the care of her husband, he would consider it more seriously. *I would be letting down the community, Mike Terrell and the rest, after they have invested in the black-smith shop and are relying upon me,* he fretted. That was not something he wanted to consider. Finding someone, an apprentice, to train or hire would be his only option. It was a problem that there weren't many young men around, and there was little actual demand for the skills of a blacksmith anymore. Most everything he did, besides an occasional wagon wheel or something minor, was farrier work. It was getting harder to make a living for a family. There were no new families coming to live in the commu-nity, and many of the young people that were there, were leaving. An idea struck him, something he hadn't thought of. *There might be someone at the encampment,* he pon-dered. *A ride over there might be worth the effort. It might actually produce an eager applicant.* He remembered see-ing some older teenage boys the last time he was there. *This might turn out to be a really good deed and a blessing for some youngster over there,* he thought. He could con-tinue to live at the hotel, and if the person he hired needed a place, they could live at the shop. Part of the salary could be room and board, in exchange for training.

With the plans for the blacksmith shop decided, he focused on Johanna's wedding. He had promised to help move her belongings to the small house, Johanna's future home.

The wedding was just a few weeks away. He would stay in the hotel with Johanna until after the wedding. He saddened a bit, as he thought about his daughter. She and her mother had planned for her marriage for a long time, making things, arranging her hope chest to take to her home one day. Now she had no hope chest, none of the items she had made or saved and put away for her own new home and life, nothing except the china. All of those things had to be burned when her mother died.

They had also left the sewing machine behind. It would have helped Johanna with everything, now and in the future. Guenther had thought it too heavy and cumbersome for the trip. That was a decision he wished he could change. He thought back to the day they crossed the Mississippi River. He remembered the family with the overloaded Conestoga that slipped off the flatboat and how they lost one of their sons to the murky water. His own wagon had crossed with ease and it is likely the sewing machine, a White Treadle, would have made it just fine. A good idea for a wedding gift; he would talk to Sara about ordering a new one from the catalog at the general store.

Later that evening when Johanna was distracted helping Etta in the kitchen, Guenther approached Sara about the order. Sara thought it was a wonderful idea, although it wouldn't arrive in time for the wedding. "It will take months before it arrives, but a sewing machine is a wonderful gift and something she will need and use, belated or not," Sara explained.

No matter the gift or the joyous occasion, Johanna didn't have her mother. Her mother was not there to be with her, to plan her wedding, to make her dress, to share in the joy. Her mother would not be there for the birth of her children. Guenther was grateful that Sara Cain had taken such an interest in Johanna, taken on the role her mother would have fulfilled in all the arrangements and planning. Sara was going to serve Johanna as her matron of honor. He was pleased about that. Johanna needed someone, a woman, to confide in and rely upon for guidance.

He puzzled for a moment, wondering about Sara and Abel. *They've been married a long time, but still had no children*, he observed. It occurred to him that, like Johanna, Sara had lost her mother recently. He remembered how Johanna fretted about her absence and the difficulty running the hotel, while she was gone to Galveston for her mother's funeral.

After the wedding, he would move to the rooms above the shop. He felt satisfied and comfortable with all his plans.

Yes sir, by this time next year, I could be a grandfather.

Chapter Twenty-eight

The big day had finally arrived. Sara Cain chased Guenther away from the suite he had shared with his daughter since their arrival. A lot had happened since that day. The most exciting thing was B.G. Steven's proposal of marriage to Johanna Gurganis. Guenther worried a bit that she was a little too young for marriage, but many girls were married at her age or younger. He knew B.G. would be good to her and that there was little need for worry. All he had to do was enjoy visits for Sunday dinner and play with grand-children as they came along.

Guenther was surprised that his Sunday suit still fit him after all these years. It didn't get very much wear, maybe a wedding or funeral every few years. He remem-bered Elizabeth fussing over his appearance when there was an occasion to dress up. Unlike his wife and daughter, the last thing Guenther wanted to do was dress up.

It was the first time that Johanna had spent an en-tire day getting dressed. She felt it a waste of time, and that she could be doing other things to prepare for the wedding and celebration afterward. She would much prefer to be busy so the time would pass faster. Sara refused to allow her out of her room, much less come downstairs to help. She had her bath and curled her hair. Her dress, her beautiful handmade dress, petticoats, stockings, shoes, and her special veil were all laid out across the bed, waiting to contribute their part to Johanna's special day.

Grateful for the gifts they'd received, Johanna made a special trip out to B.G.'s house to put them away. There would probably be more gifts after the wedding, and she knew a trip back into town in a few days would be necessary. She would need to collect the last of her things and whatever gifts there were. Sara had promised to set them aside until she could come to town.

Johanna had tried to start over with her hope chest and had managed to accumulate a few things with the money Sara paid her for working. Her mother's china stayed in storage at the hotel. It wouldn't be moved until they were in the house to stay. She had refused to leave it in an empty house in the country.

Johanna was feeling embarrassed about coming back into town a few days after their wedding night. Most everyone would know. She would too, by then. Her questions would have been answered. Sara haltingly tried to explain what to expect and to answer Johanna's questions. Sara wasn't as comfortable discussing it as she'd thought she would be. Mostly, Johanna took away that the act was a very private thing between a husband and wife, and she understood that what would happen on her wedding night was part of being a wife. She loved B.G. and would do whatever was necessary to be a good wife.

The wedding was a blur. The ceremony, performed by Reverend Luke Matthews, was brief, but beautiful. Once again, at the celebration afterward, Johanna and B.G. circled the floor dance after dance, just like the night they first met. Neither of them had an appetite for the dinner that had been prepared by Etta and the ladies from the community.

The guests enjoyed a wonderful meal, dancing and visiting. They were encouraged to stay as long as they liked. However, the newlyweds had a long trip out to their house. Many of the guests lingered to visit, dance and party most of the night, but Johanna and B.G. left in a wagon that had been decorated with twine and ribbons streaming behind it. Attached were all sorts of cans, tins, old boots, a slop jar and whatever the ranch hands could gather to embarrass B.G.

As soon as they were out of sight of the wedding guests, and the community, B.G. stopped the wagon, turned to Johanna and passionately kissed her. Except for one brief moment, when she and Guenther had come out to the ranch, he had waited from the first day he laid eyes on her, to hold her so tightly, to kiss her, to make her his own. He set the horses at a brisk canter and held Johanna in his arms all the way home.

Approaching their dark house, B.G. lit a lantern to escort Johanna inside.

Johanna's heart was in her throat. She was so much in love with her new husband she had to hold back tears. B.G. was every bit as nervous as his new wife.

Johanna stepped into the bedroom, closing the door behind her. She removed her wedding dress and slipped into her gown. Pulling back the coverlet, she discovered the lovely new bedding that had been ordered from the *Dream Book*, a surprise gift for her. Easing into the bed, she quietly waited for B.G. to enter.

The door slowly opened. B.G.'s silhouette was illuminated from the lantern light behind him. The sight awakened Johanna to unfamiliar feelings. His arms went quickly around her. Breathless, Johanna was both surprised and shocked. It all happened quickly, but she was thrilled by what had just occurred. Happiness flooded over her with the realization that she was finally, completely a woman and his wife.

Johanna spent the next few days enjoying her new home, appreciating all the work her husband had done as a gift for her. The bed, the chifferobe, the cabinets for her china, and such nice linens for their bed, all made her feel content and happy. She busied herself arranging the house like she wanted it, working in the garden and learning to cook on the small wood stove, which would take some time, she'd discovered. Being the lady of the house was a new experience.

In the days that passed she began to know the pleasure of their union. She looked forward to her husband's return home each evening.

Johanna's questions had been answered. She was no longer curious and apprehensive. But now, she was more embarrassed than ever to go back to the hotel for her things, to face everyone. *They are going to know,* she thought.

Chapter Twenty-nine

Western expansion continued with immigration from other countries and migration from eastern states. People flooded to America, many of them headed west. Various government programs and legislation had been enacted to accommodate and draw settlers to the frontier.

One way or another, after being forced from their homelands, the peaceful American Indians were then pushed from their reservations to areas even less hospitable, or forced to dissolve their reservations altogether. Having little or no understanding or concern for the plight of the Indians, the settlers continued to come. Those Indians who resisted were considered savages or renegades and were imprisoned or eventually killed in the many battles that followed.

The settlers came for the same reasons they had been coming for many years, because of overcrowding, joblessness, expensive land prices and the search for wealth. In the case of many immigrants, they came to escape oppression and for the desire of a better life. They came because of stories they'd heard or because of land companies that lured them with promises of good deals and success. Some came because they already worked for the companies that owned the railroads, and in later years, they came because of oil. They came because of their belief in Manifest Destiny, and they came from everywhere.

After the transcontinental railroad and other railroads were constructed, the settlers came by railroad, by wagon, horseback and stagecoach. Sometimes they came on foot. Those who had the financial means often depended on guide companies to take them to their destinations.

Ayers Guide Company had been taking settlers West for many years. Before he and a partner had formed the company, Eli Ayers had taken families to destinations beyond the Mississippi River, across the plains, to Texas, Arkansas, even to California. His company had begun to specialize in the Oklahoma Territory. He and his partner worked with a government agency and knew the ins and outs of the programs that were available to the settlers.

The trips by the Ayers Guide Company to Oklahoma Territory were conducted by multiple methods. Most were a combination of rail and wagon. A group of settlers could travel by rail to a specific destination, and then continue by wagon to areas beyond the reach of the railroad. Few of those early settlements or communities survived for very long without rail service.

Eli's company was successful. His customers were always satisfied with the efficient manner in which their travels were conducted. Much of his business was due to referrals. Less adventurous settlers, potential merchants and tradesmen usually preferred a more dignified approach to claiming or buying land or lots, while others were more willing to brave the elements and strike out on their own.

A homesteader could sometimes lay claim to a parcel of land, live on it and develop it until it officially became his. These and other actions would fall under one of the many programs enacted throughout the period of settlement of the Oklahoma Territory, or Indian Lands.

At one point, several of the reservations were broken up and divided among the inhabitants and potential settlers, thereby dissolving the reservations. The existence of the reservations interfered with westward expansion. The Indians suffered the consequences of much coercion and corruption.

Eli's efficient service was the result of careful planning, exploration and years of experience. He carefully scouted his routes, knowing good places to camp, where there was water, safe passage, abundant wildlife and other towns or settlements along the way.

An extra hand accompanied him now. While there were fewer Indian worries, there were more outlaws and sometimes rowdy, anxious folks, even from within his group of travelers. Still handsome, Eli was every bit the agile, rugged individual he had always been, but even so, he didn't care to conduct the guide trips alone anymore.

Ayer's Guide Company advertised through ads in newspapers and bulletins posted at railway stations, telegraph offices and land offices. The ads, or leaflets, always offered detailed information about routes, restrictions and requirements such as the equipment and supplies that would be needed, as well as the approximate estimation of days on the trail. They also stated a specific destination, often leaving a group to continue on without a guide after reaching the destination. The company had recently received prior notification that town sites had been set aside for the creation of county seats in Oklahoma. Cities were going to be open for settlement by auctions for town lots. The destination for the next guide service for a group of merchants was Fort Sill and a town soon to be named Lawton, in Comanche County, Oklahoma.

Chapter Thirty

Without her wagon and Rosie, a heartbroken and shaken Cheri didn't know what to do or which way to turn. Why that Indian didn't let the others hurt her she would never know. *Maybe I was going to be next, and Rosie just happened to be closer to them at the wrong time.* The sight of Rosie being pulled and pushed, stripped of her clothing and pawed by those animals was sickening. Every time she closed her eyes the vision crept back into her mind. Worse still, she felt guilty because she survived unscathed, while Rosie suffered so terribly. Thinking of all their possessions and wagon being looted and burned was more than she could bear. *How do I start over? Where do I go? What do I do now?*

Once Dodge hadn't found the saddlebags in the burned-out wagon, he didn't think of them again. There had been too much happening and he had finally given up any hope of ever finding them. But there they were, lying across the back of one of the horses that hadn't run off during the ruckus. When he saw them, his first reaction was disbelief. It was too good to be true. He slowly walked toward the horse, methodically slipped the saddlebags off, flipped them open and slowly inserted his hand into the deep warm leather. Miraculously, when he withdrew his hand, there it was at last, the Cain's money, four straps of twenty-dollar silver certificates.

Dodge hadn't thought about what to do next or where they would go. Cheri had to be escorted somewhere. Leaving without her was out of the question. All she had done for three days was cry. He knew the tears would eventually begin to dry up. They would talk then.

Reed and Jackson hesitated to leave them out in the desert alone. They had ridden over to the nearby settlement, returning with water and food. Dodge was grateful to finally have a meal. It had been several days since he'd had anything but jerky. They suggested that moving over to the settlement for a few days would be safer than staying there on the ridge, but Cheri refused to go.

Finally, on the morning of the fifth day after her ordeal, Cheri awoke early and seemed almost like her old self again. "Dodge, I need to bathe. Please take me to the springs over there, please," she begged. "Then take me in to the settlement so I can find something clean to wear or wash these clothes. Then, if you will, I want you take me to Fort Sill. Rosie and I were going there. I still need to go. I can find work there."

Cheri took off her clothes and slipped into the water. "Oh my, this is cold!" Dodge had seen Cheri without her clothes before. She didn't hesitate to disrobe in front of him. Her smooth, clear skin and shapely body was perfect. His thoughts flashed back to better days when he'd indulged himself in the pink ruffled wagon. Cheri had always been his favorite.

They found some boys' pants and a shirt for Cheri at the settlement. There wasn't much there to choose from, but she would rather wear anything than the clothes she had. She made Dodge help her burn them. With her hair pulled up under a hat, and wearing boy's pants, Cheri actually looked like a young kid. They bought a saddle for the horse that the Indians had left behind, the one that didn't run away, the one that was carrying the saddlebags, money and other plunder.

Once again, Reed and Jackson parted company with Dodge Blackburn. They were on their way to Austin, another of their many trips, another time they'd crossed paths with Dodge Blackburn. After hearing Dodge's story, they were going to check in with Texas Ranger Dred Hill as soon as they arrived there. They assured Dodge that the papers they were carrying would clear all of them of any suspicion.

Those cowboys said their goodbyes to Dodge and Cheri. They were going to head to the encampment on their way to Austin, maybe spend a few nights there. It would be their first time back there since all the trouble.

Dodge set out, once again, in unfamiliar territory. He wasn't alone this time. Cherie was good company. She was confident and smart on the trail, and wasn't afraid of anything, other than Indian renegades. She had seen a lot and had learned to be pretty tough in her short life, but she didn't act tough. *She seems so nice. Not at all like someone who's had a hard life,* Dodge found himself thinking. He was seeing her in a different light. He admitted to himself that he was quite fond of her, acknowledging they'd probably had similar lives.

Cheri hadn't questioned Dodge about how he happened to show up in the middle of nowhere to rescue them. He didn't offer an explanation.

The Cain's money had finally been recovered. Now, what to do? He had been gone a long time, and didn't know whether he wanted to go back or not. It had never occurred to him to not go back home, until now.

Oklahoma offered a lot of opportunity. He could lay claim to some of the free land or buy some of the railroad land that was being sold cheap, maybe a dollar or so an acre, he'd heard. The railroads had acquired millions of acres of land by hook or crook. They were now offering that land at low prices. Their goal was to further populate the plains by creating more passengers and shipping for themselves. Maybe it was time for him to take advantage of that opportunity to make a life for himself, a life independent of the Cain's.

Composing it in his head, Dodge planned a letter to send to Sara Cain explaining almost everything. He apologized for his unexplained absence. He explained about losing and recovering the money, but not the details about how it was lost. He expressed the need to make a loan of the money to himself, because for now, his plan was to remain in Oklahoma.

He wouldn't mention Cheri. That explanation wouldn't be easy to put on paper, nor something Sara would understand.

With some of that money, Cheri might be able to buy some land, too, maybe find a husband or start a new business. But she needed help getting a new start, doing something different than she had in the past.

Dodge had money in the bank in Austin and would send a letter to Sara authorizing the bank to give her enough to repay the loan. She would receive more information about how to correspond with him as soon as he knew. He would end the letter with one last request, "Sara, please send my love to your parents." The letter would be composed and mailed as soon as he found a flat surface, a piece of paper on which to write, and a town with a post office.

As he and Cheri rode out toward Oklahoma, Dodge looked back over his shoulder to see Reed and

Jackson disappear. Their sincere words on parting were still ringing in his ears, "Hey, ever going back to Sandy Creek? Hope we see you again."

Chapter Thirty-one

Mike Terrell had a special fondness for the old Murphy chuck wagon. It had been stored in a shed on the ranch for a long time. Its day had come and gone, since the long cattle drives of the past had been replaced by the railroads. Once a railhead had been established in San Antonio, the old chuck wagon had been put to rest. The Terrell cattle were driven to San Antonio, which took little more than a week, maybe two. There were small communities and towns along the way, hardly worth the effort of hiring a cook and breaking out and stocking up the Murphy.

The cross breeding efforts on the Terrell Ranch had finally paid off. Though small by earlier standards, a good size herd of the Longhorn mix had been developed. A rancher from the Stockman's Association in Nebraska had an interest in the crossbred cattle. Disregarding Mike's suggestion that the heavier, beefier cattle wouldn't travel well, the rancher insisted that the cattle be driven over land rather than forced into cattle cars and delivered by rail.

There were no long drives like that anymore, but it was a reasonable enough request.

The drive would be more difficult than in past years. Open range had diminished, as many farms had sprung up throughout the state, and more pastures and ranch lands were fenced, usually with barbed wire.

A team would have to go ahead to scout the old Western Trail for clear passage and to make arrangements with property owners and Indian reservations. Fulfilling the request was possible, but difficult, and it would take a long time. It was unlikely the herd could move more than ten miles a day. The trail boss estimated as long as six or seven months if all went well.

Mike was glad for an opportunity to sell the herd. It was time for him to start cutting back and clearing out the livestock. It was time to think about the future of the ranch and the transfer of ownership to the university.

He had given a lot of thought to the subject and decided to move off the ranch, maybe to Austin, to spend his later years. A friend owned a hotel in Austin and he could be pretty comfortable there. At least he would be able to make sure the transfer went according to the estate plan, rather than letting it wait until after his death. It would take a few years to accomplish his goals, and that would be just about right.

Mike knew that his move would mean that B.G. would have to find his own ranch. He'd had the opportunity to develop a small herd on his little place there on the ranch. He had a wife now, and would soon be starting a family. It was time he got established some place permanent. Some of his cattle were being sold along with Mike's. That would give him and Johanna a good start.

Mike had sent word to Guenther that the Murphy needed some repairs. That work completed, the wagon was ready to go. After the drive, Mike would put the old Murphy wagon up for sale, along with the other equipment, but he would keep all that information to himself.

The hands were preparing the herd, rounding them up, dipping and branding the cattle. They would be ready to go within the week.

Assembled in front of the ranch house, the new trail boss, Mitch Ray, B.G., Tony the cook, and the rest of the drovers listened to Mike's final words of encouragement and instruction.

"Move 'em out!"

Mike stood on his porch and watched as the cattle slowly moved along right in front of the ranch house, right through the front gate. They crossed the road, avoiding the bridge, and walked through the fresh clean water of Sandy Creek. There hadn't been a cattle drive north out of Texas for ten years or more. They were going to catch the old Western Trail north through Texas, cross the Red River near old Doan's Crossing, through Oklahoma Territory, and on to Dodge City. Crossing through Oklahoma Territory was going to require maneuvering the patchy remains of the Indian reservation that had been opened up to settlers. Taking a herd across the Red River, which occasionally shifted its banks during heavy rains and could be dotted with quicksand, would be a real concern.

The plan was to meet up at Dodge City with the rancher from Nebraska who had purchased the cattle. Once the cattle were handed off, the cowboys' job would be done. B.G. and some of the others would return to the Terrell Ranch. The trail boss, cook and remaining drovers would go their own way. Mike Terrell had been lucky to find cowboys who would still trail a herd of cattle, but when they were done, he wouldn't need them anymore.

80C8

A layover at The Flat gave the drovers a few days rest, each taking their turn staying with the herd. "The Flat" offered entertainment and the opportunity to replenish supplies. The Clear Fork branch of the Brazos River flowed nearby, providing water for the cattle and a good place to rest. Frequently visited by unsavory characters in the past, the history of its glory days offered accounts of famous characters like Doc Holiday and Wyatt Earp. Close by, Fort Griffin had long ago been decommissioned. The soldiers there used to help serve as local law enforcement. It appeared there was no official law around. The drovers could have quickly found themselves in a compromising situation. Mitch Ray didn't allow the men to stay in town overnight, just in case.

B.G. spent almost every moment of the drive thinking about his new wife. Seldom far from his thoughts were the nights they shared. He had waited what seemed like an eternity to have her, only to have to leave. His nights and days were spent longing for his sweet Johanna.

B.G. forfeited visiting the saloon and bathhouse, but he was assigned the task of driving the wagon into town to pick up supplies with the cook. While patiently leaning against a doorway, he recognized a familiar figure, riding beside a young boy. No, it was a young woman. To his amazement, it was Dodge Blackburn. "Dodge, Dodge Blackburn!" B.G. called out to Dodge and Cheri, but they kept riding. They rode out of town and out of sight. B.G. couldn't pursue them in the wagon full of supplies. *What is he doing all the way out here? Who was that woman?*

B.G. dropped a letter at the post office before they rode back out to the herd.

Lying at the bottom of the post office box at The Flat were two letters, both addressed to the care of the Cain Hotel and General Store.

Chapter Thirty-two

The streets emptied early. People had gone home to batten down for the storm. Henry Freeze stepped outside his store to close and fasten the shutters over the windows and doors. A quick trip upstairs, where they'd always lived, accomplished the same thing, shutters closed and latched. The wind had kicked up a bit and it had rained off and on all day. The Weather Bureau had put out the double square hurricane warning flags.

The Freeze General Store had closed every day at 5:30 p.m. for as long as they had been in business. That day, Henry turned the closed sign around at 5:00 p.m.

Going through the usual routine of closing out his register, organizing the inventory, restocking shelves and sweeping the floor, Henry reminisced about all the days that he had performed that same routine, about the years they had operated the store together as a family. Sara's departure, after her marriage, left a hole in their day-to-day routine, and of course in their hearts. Katherine's death had taken the joy out of everything that they had previously shared. He didn't have the same interest in the store anymore. The pride and the joy were gone. The ambition to be successful had passed. In a blink, his future was behind him.

"I believe it's time to put a for sale sign on the door, old girl!" Henry spoke out loud as he looked around the store. "I won't tell Sara yet. She'll just start in about me coming to the Hill Country. Maybe going out there wouldn't be so bad. At least I can help them with their business. They can always bring me back here when the time comes. She's been begging me to sell for years. I guess maybe it's time."

At 6:00 p. m. Henry Freeze turned off the lights and went upstairs.

෴

News of the hurricane spread across Texas quickly. Galveston had been destroyed. Thousands of people had perished. Sara was frantic to hear from her father. Little or no communication was coming out of the devastation that was once the island city.

"Abel, I have to go, we must go! I have to find my father, find out if he is okay."

Reasoning with Sara was almost impossible, but he finally convinced her that there was no place to go. The city was basically gone. "We have to hold tight and wait."

Somewhat isolated in their location, they had to wait for the rider from Austin who brought the mail and newspaper. The *Galveston Daily News* had somehow managed to publish an account of the devastation and it was duplicated in the Austin paper.

Each day and moment that passed without word from her father, each news account that reached them, began to convince Sara that not only had her father not survived, but like so many others, would never be found.

Most of the city was leveled. Thousands of people were killed or never found. Some were never identified. Many were cremated or buried in mass graves.

The Freeze General Store, along with all the other destruction, was eventually scrapped and hauled away.

Sara had hoped and waited for word that never came. It was a miracle that her father had made all those financial arrangements at the time he did, and how fortunate that everything had been transferred to the Austin lawyer and the bank, also in Austin. It was almost as if he'd had a premonition. She had personally delivered all of the papers to the lawyer after her mother died. *The lawyer will know what to do. We'll plan a trip to Austin.*

Coming to terms with the reality was overwhelming. Sara was hardly able to make it through each day. Abel tried to console her, but his efforts were futile. Both of her parents were gone, and their store, even the city. Overcome by the horror that her father and all the people in Galveston witnessed and endured, Sara sought Luke Matthews for prayer and comfort. Thank God for Luke. He was always there when she needed him.

Sara wondered if Dodge knew about the hurricane. *Surely, the news has traveled everywhere.* She had received only one letter from Dodge and had no idea how to notify him about her father. He still didn't know about her mother. It had been so long since she had heard from him. She hoped that this terrible news might prompt him to contact her. In his last and only letter, he had promised to let her know how to reach him. She was still waiting. There was much he needed to know.

Chapter Thirty-three

There were too many people who wandered freely about the land. Johanna couldn't feel comfortable leaving their belongings unattended at their isolated little house on the ranch. With B.G. and all the other hands gone on the cattle drive, Mike was staying in town, too, at the hotel most of the time. The ranch was virtually deserted, but Johanna still needed to feed and water the chickens, gather the eggs and water the garden.

Although not daily, she was still working for Sara, and she was trying to stay in both places a few days each. Since her father had moved out of their former suite to the room above the blacksmith shop, the suite was no longer available to her. In Dodge's absence, Sara insisted Johanna make use of his room when she was in town for work. Working for Sara and staying in Dodge's room at the hotel helped keep her from feeling quite so lonely. It was also helpful to be near her father, and good to receive B.G.'s frequent letters, mailed whenever he passed near a town with postal service.

Johanna hadn't told anyone, but she had felt sick ever since B.G. left. At first she didn't have any suspicions, but then her flow didn't come, and hadn't come for several months. She kept her secret, knowing that everyone would have to be told very soon.

Rather than take the buckboard, Johanna rode Pebble on her trips back and forth. Riding him was much faster. Having him with her made her feel a little safer, though she didn't worry much about her safety. She was a good shot with both a rifle and a pistol. She and B.G. even had target practice before he left on the cattle drive. Mike rode out with her occasionally and would go on over to check on the ranch and stock. He also needed to check on the housekeeper and the few hands that were still there.

Johanna could feel a flutter in her lower abdomen. She knew it must be the baby. It made her giddy to think about being a mother and caring for a baby, hers and B.G.'s baby. Strangely, she felt calm, though a little frightened, when considering that one day soon she would give birth.

Johanna needed Sara's help to let out a few of her dresses. She knew that she wouldn't be able to work after her secret began to show. It was time to tell Sara.

Sara had noticed that Johanna appeared to have gained weight and fully suspected that she might be carrying a baby. Always kind and loving, she hugged Johanna as she heard the news.

The good seamstress that she was, Sara knew just how to enlarge Johanna's clothes. They also looked through dress patterns and fabric there at the store. Johanna had admired a particular bolt of fabric. At Sara's urging, she happily selected it and a pattern.

A White Treadle sewing machine, just like her mother's, was a total surprise one morning when she returned to the store. To her joy, Guenther was present that morning to proudly bestow the belated wedding present.

Johanna stayed at the hotel a few extra days that week. With Sara's help, she altered her dresses and made a new one. The next project would be baby clothes, so they looked at baby patterns and fabric, also.

Johanna began looking through the catalogs for baby things. Guenther insisted on making the crib for his first grandchild. The next few months would pass quickly. She would be very busy making a mattress for the crib, blankets and diapers. Deciding that she was going to be a modern mother, she ordered baby bottles from the catalog.

Johanna knew the day would come when she would have to go into town and stay until the baby was born. There was no doctor, but there were mothers nearby who knew how to birth a baby and would surely help.

B.G.'s letters came regularly. The drive was moving slowly. Unfortunately, never knowing exactly where he was, it wasn't possible to get letters to him. His letters told exciting tales. Some of the stories told of his frustration and some were even frightening. Many days were being spent waiting for agreements with farmers and ranchers so they could cross their land. Long detours were taking extra time. His most recent letter described the problems at the Red River. He confirmed their earlier concerns that the Red River crossing might be treacherous. It had surprised him that they actually encountered quicksand. They'd even had to pull a few steers out of it.

B.G. mentioned another surprise; seeing Dodge Blackburn in a small town named The Flat. He'd been unable to speak with him, as he was riding out of town with a young woman and didn't hear him call out to them.

The cattle drive had taken longer than expected. It had been just over eight months, but B.G.'s last letter was mailed from Dodge City. The cattle were being held just outside of town waiting for the rancher with his drovers from Nebraska. Once the bill of sale was completed, B.G. would be on his way home.

The time had come for Johanna to move into town. With B.G.'s absence it was even more necessary than ever. She had wanted to wait, hoping that B.G. would be home any day, but her father and Sara insisted that she take the wagon on this trip and return with her belongings.

∞∞

BANG, BANG, BANG.

Sara and Abel ran out the front door of the general store. The loud noise had spooked the horses that were tied to the post out front. The local dogs were barking and howling. People nearby came out to see if someone was shooting off fireworks or a gun, right in the middle of town. The loud noise had alarmed everyone.

BANG, BANG, BANG. It was one of those new motorcars. The drummer, who stopped by from time to time selling his goods and wares, had arrived that day in one of those new machines, the back seat loaded down with merchandise for the store. None of the residents had actually seen a motorcar before that day, except in a newspaper or magazine.

A curious crowd gathered around the spectacle. Mike Terrell strolled out of the hotel cafe to see what caused all the commotion. His usual cool demeanor was still intact, but a closer look would have exposed the boyish desire to own one of the motorcars. He even liked the smell of the exhaust that exploded out the back end. He approached the salesman and asked to accompany him on a ride. Seeing an opportunity to possibly make a commission, the drummer agreed to Mike's request.

Off they went, Mike and the drummer, down the bumpy road and out into the countryside. It seemed that the drummer might be selling motorcars now. Actually, there was a shop in San Antonio that ordered and put the machines together. The drummer was not the first to have one.

It didn't take any selling for Mike. He was already planning on how B.G. would go to San Antonio to pick one up for him. B.G. would have to learn to drive it. Then he could bring it to the ranch and teach Mike how to drive.

The streets of San Antonio, as well as those in other major cities, were littered with horse-drawn wagons, motorcars, electric bicycles, horses and more. It was a mishmash of past and present, as was everything at the turn of the century. There were no streets or paved roads in the Hill Country like there were in the city. There were mostly rutted wagon trails. Texas had fallen behind other states in road building. At the time, counties were responsible for building the roads, and many counties had limited funds. Work on the roads had been accomplished with volunteers and consisted mostly of removing stumps. But none of that made any difference to Mike.

He decided the machine fit perfectly in his future plans for living in the city. He imagined living at a hotel, taking trips, traveling all around Texas with no need to stable a horse. There were only a few motorcars in all of Texas and he was going to be among the first to have one.

All the arrangements were made through the drummer. The order would be placed as soon as he returned to San Antonio. There was still no telephone service available at the Terrell ranch, so Mike insisted that a telegram be sent the minute the motorcar was ready.

Guenther hadn't left his shop to see about the commotion, but stood in the doorway quietly observing. He was a little less enthused about the scene and about the machine. He stood quietly accepting the realization that he was witnessing the end of an era.

Chapter Thirty-four

Fort Sill was huge. The area around the fort when Dodge and Cheri arrived was packed with wagons and carts and horses and settlers and Indians. There were tents scattered everywhere. People had been gathering for days in the hot August weather, waiting for the auction to begin.

Dodge and Cheri were some of the lucky ones. They had a covered wagon, purchased before they crossed the border into Oklahoma. Many people had come by train and had no other transportation or cover to protect them from the heat.

Dodge and Cheri were there to make their bid, the same as all the others. There were over a thousand people there to bid on the lots being auctioned to the highest bidder.

Cheri and Rosie's big plans to come to Oklahoma to find work, and maybe a husband, were gone. Cheri didn't have her friend to work and live with anymore. She was nervous, but Dodge had persuaded her that they should bid on the lots, and if they succeeded, he would help her open a business. He assured her that he had enough money to accomplish both.

They scouted out the township carefully. They argued over which site might be the best, which street would end up being the most heavily traveled. Dodge could imagine the street lined with businesses, buildings and sidewalks. Cheri could imagine chairs and flowerpots and a pretty door with decorative glass cutouts and display windows.

A corner lot would be expensive. A lot in the middle or the end of a street would probably go for less, but would have too much traffic. The perfect lot for a general store or a millinery store would be the second lot from the end, on the busiest street. The lots had been surveyed and roped off, so they selected three lots that fit their specifications. They would bid on all three, hoping they would get one.

Carefully calculating the amount of money to spend on the lot, the amount to build a building, the amount to stock a store and the amount that would be needed to sustain the business until it could support itself, Dodge's head was full of numbers.

If anyone knew how to manage a new business from ground up it was Dodge. He had worked for Henry Freeze most of his life and helped Sara and Abel with their store from the ground up. He also knew how to manage the money, and knew they would have what they needed.

Before they even broke ground he already had plans in his head about how to construct the building, two stories with an upstairs residence for Cheri. Dodge was gratified that Cheri had embraced the idea of owning and running a store. She had proved that she was smart and accomplished and easily picked up whatever he taught her. It had been his intention to stay until she could manage on her own. Once she was on her feet and the business was successful, he would move on, seeking out new challenges. Dodge had discovered that he was at his best when he was faced with a challenge. He had followed through with everything except letting Sara know that he was in Lawton, Oklahoma.

He still needed to write to Sara, if for no other reason than to let her know he still didn't have an official address. Lawton, Oklahoma, the proposed name of the new township where the lots were being auctioned, was where he hoped to create a new business and help Cheri with a new start in life. A post office was already designated for the town.

It was the news of the Galveston hurricane that made him want to reach out to Sara. According to stories he'd heard and newspaper reports, he knew there wasn't anything he could have done to help. He knew he couldn't leave Cheri yet. His only choice was to wait. Maybe when he had an address and sent it to Sara, she would let him know more. Surely Abel went as soon as it was allowed. It broke his heart to know what Henry and Katherine may have suffered. Unaware of Katherine's earlier heart attack and death, he felt certain they didn't make it through the storm. He was ashamed that so much time had passed before he heard about it, that he was out in the middle of nowhere chasing saddlebags because he'd been irresponsible. He was ashamed that he hadn't heard and gone to Galveston immediately to come to their aid, if possible. *It hardly makes any difference now. Henry and Katherine are most likely dead, and after all that has happened, Sara and Abel probably have no use for me...probably don't ever want to see the likes of me again.*

The auction went on all day in the heat. Dodge bid each time when their numbers came up. Finally, the bidding on the last lot, the best one, dropped off early and Dodge and Cheri won the bid and won the lot.

Cheri threw her arms around Dodge and kissed him square on the lips. He shook his head, then grabbed her and hugged her tightly and kissed her right back. Their celebrating went on all evening. They shared a drink or two or three of whisky and their evening turned into a long night of lovemaking, finally responding to the electricity that had been between them ever since Dodge saved her from that terrible fate, and ever since Cheri had disrobed in front of him at San Solomon Springs. For the first time

ever, Cheri lost herself totally in the arms of a man, Dodge
Blackburn.

Chapter Thirty-five

Johanna was grateful that everything seemed to be in order when she arrived at her home. She pulled the buckboard into the barn, unhitched and fed the horses. Then she fed the chickens and began gathering the eggs. "Oh!" Johanna jumped as a chicken snake slithered off one of the straw nests. Scrambling to keep her balance, but unable to because of her swollen belly, she fell backward over the door facing. Her head hit the rocky ground with a solid thud. Stunned and briefly unable to move, she lay there waiting to determine the damage. Just as she attempted to roll over, she felt warmth gush between her legs. Stricken by severe pain, she fainted. Regaining consciousness, she discovered her skirt was wet and tinged with blood. She struggled to her feet and managed to get into the house and onto the bed. The sun sat that evening and rose the next morning to the screams of Johanna Steven, while her body bore the ravages of childbirth, alone.

Awake again, after fainting several times from the gripping pain, she discovered her baby, still attached to the umbilical cord, lying silently between her legs. Instinctively, she gathered him up and gently shook and patted him until he began to gasp and cry. She had no knowledge of childbirth, but somehow knew that she must cut that cord and detach it from herself. She got out of the bed and carried the baby with her to the kitchen where she got a knife and cut through the cord. Then she tore a piece of cloth and tied it around him holding the end of the cord against his tummy. She gathered the strength to get a pail and go outside for water. Johanna washed her baby and cleaned herself. Holding the infant closely, she slipped back into bed, pulling the covers over them both. Johanna and her tiny baby cried themselves to sleep.

When the expected day of Johanna's return had come and gone, Sara and Guenther became alarmed. Knowing there must be trouble, they were fearful there had been an accident.

They took the big wagon in case they might need it. Guenther harnessed four horses for a speedy trip. He was in a hurry and wasn't going to waste any time. He and Sara took the shortest route to the house, rather than go through the ranch. They were not prepared for what they would find.

There was no sound coming from the dark house. It looked empty, so Guenther pushed open the unlocked door. He knew immediately from the mess everywhere that Johanna was in distress. Sara rushed into the bedroom, finding both of them asleep, but Johanna more unconscious than asleep, and burning up with fever. They took the baby, who appeared to be well, from her arms. Guenther ran to the well for water and they began bathing Johanna with the cool water to get her fever down. Neither Sara nor Guenther knew for certain what needed to be done, and the baby had begun to cry. Sara diapered him and rummaged through the few drawers in the chifferobe for swaddling.

A very timely blessing appeared in the doorway. The housekeeper and one of the ranch hands saw the unfamiliar wagon and stopped to check on all of the activity at the house. The housekeeper took over, knowing exactly what to do. Within a few hours, Johanna was awake, her fever had begun to subside, she was clean, and in a fresh gown and bed. Baby Joe was having a bottle of goat's milk. His mother's breasts were engorged and hot from infection, but had been packed with compresses. Fortunately, Johanna had decided to be a modern mother and had those bottles washed and ready for use.

The next surprise to appear in the doorway was a relieved but awestruck B.G. Steven! He had stopped by the hotel and blacksmith shop, only to be told that Sara and Guenther had left town in search of his wife. He was terrified that something had happened to Johanna. After all those days and nights and months on a horse, he rode as hard and fast as he could to his little house on the ranch. He was fearful every step of the way that his wife was injured or dead.

It was all too much for one very tired young man to take in at once. When he left on the cattle drive he had a new wife, now he had a wife and baby. B.G. was speechless, but the happiest young man alive. Johanna was fine and they had a baby. On his knees beside the bed, he and Johanna held each other and their new baby. Together they cried and marveled at their new son, Joseph Guenther Steven.

Chapter Thirty-six

He was a grandfather at last. Guenther couldn't believe his good fortune. "A grandson, Joseph Guenther Steven, named after me." He was a little worried about the baby's tiny size, but he seemed healthy, his color was good and he had a good set of lungs.

"What a boy," Guenther exclaimed. He couldn't wait to go back out to see him.

Guenther was more worried about Johanna. He didn't fully understand the complication and knew she'd improved, but her color wasn't good and she was stooped as if she was still in pain, although she insisted she wasn't. He was certain he saw her wince from time to time. He suspected she had hurt her back in the fall, but didn't want to worry B.G. or anyone else. She probably needed to see a doctor.

ഇൻ

The will and estate plan had provided for Mike to live on the ranch for his whole life. The news that he'd decided to move off the ranch and start the process early was certainly hard to hear. It would be a financial burden on the young couple and new parents. It meant they had to move as well. Guenther also knew about the loss B.G. took on the sale of the cattle and was aware of the salary he would lose once Mike was gone. Above all, Guenther wouldn't have the Terrell ranch business anymore. That would be a blow to his blacksmith shop.

Guenther's attempt to find an apprentice had failed. When he went to the encampment to search for a potential candidate, he discovered that the few eligible young men who lived there had left a long time ago. They had joined the military to fight the Spaniards in Cuba. That left him with no one. Guenther really wanted to retire, especially after the birth of baby Joe. He wanted to spend time with his grandson and somehow help his daughter and son-in-law.

He thought back to the day he'd found a notice on the bulletin board at the telegraph office in Memphis. There were still plenty of people coming to Texas. He could do the same thing, send a notice to post at the telegraph office in Memphis, but he would send them everywhere, to every major city. A visit to the telegraph office was in order. There would be a buyer out there somewhere. He would sell the shop and spend that money and his retirement helping his family.

The only problem with finding a buyer, in this day and time, was that there was so little need for blacksmiths anymore. A farrier, maybe, but even at that, blacksmithing would hardly support a family. Guenther knew that motorcars were going to completely replace the use of horses and wagons in just a matter of time.

The closest telegraph office was an hour away. He would go in the morning, so he could be back before dusk.

St. Louis, Memphis, Little Rock, Dodge City, New Orleans, the list was long, but Guenther was serious about the endeavor. That blacksmith shop, along with all the equipment, was officially for sale.

It was early when Guenther walked across the street for breakfast. Sara hardly had breakfast ready. Over a cup of coffee Guenther stood in the doorway to the kitchen and discussed his concerns about Johanna and B.G. and Baby Joe. Mike's decision had everyone in the community puzzled, but few realized the impact it was going to have on B.G. and Johanna. He wanted Sara to know the shop would be closed for the day while he traveled to the telegraph office. He was also going by to visit Johanna and Baby Joe before he came home, and he hadn't wanted her to worry about his absence. He also shared the information about his final decision to sell the shop.

Sara couldn't hide her disappointment. She certainly hoped Guenther could find a buyer. Her fear was that the shop would close, and another business and family would be moving away. When it was discovered that the railroad wasn't going to lay tracks nearby, Sara knew it would be difficult for the community to survive. Even with Sandy Creek and the Llano River at their fingertips, the railroad made a big difference for any community. The railroad would have brought businesses and families. It worried her to see any business close or any family leave.

Even though Pebble always resisted, Guenther hitched him to the wagon. He had been in the stable for several weeks without any exercise. Johanna had taken the wagon on her last trip out to the ranch and hadn't returned due to Baby Joe's birth. Pebble had been confined to the stable ever since. "You may as well settle your feisty self down, my friend, you need the exercise."

Pebble continued to fight the reins and harness, but Guenther was determined. He hitched only two horses for the trip, Grace and Pebble. Grace was a calm, dependable workhorse, and Pebble, a spirited, spoiled brat.

Chapter Thirty-seven

It would take a while before a motorcar would be available for Mike, but the last thing B.G. wanted to hear was a request from Mike to go anywhere. His bones still ached from that long troublesome trail drive. He didn't want to leave Johanna and Baby Joe for such nonsense and extravagance. He loved Mike, and of course he would go when the time came, but he had other troubling things on his mind right now.

In hindsight he realized that he should never have agreed to go on the long arduous trail drive. He couldn't imagine that they had made any money after all was said and done. In fact, they hadn't. It had occurred to him that Mike really didn't care whether he made any money from that sale, rather that he was flattered that someone wanted his crossbred longhorns. It was obvious that Mike's priorities had changed. When B.G. confronted Mike he was stunned to have his suspicions confirmed. It was Mike's intention to liquidate the herd, sell all the equipment and move off the ranch. He estimated it would take a few years, but the university would be taking over the ranch very soon.

Two years would give B.G. enough time to find a place and move his family, but he felt let down. He'd spent so much time and effort on his little home, thinking he would be living there a lot longer. Although knowing it would never belong to him, he thought he'd have the time to benefit from it in other ways. He hadn't really made any money to speak of, much less made any on the cattle he took to Dodge City along with Mike's. Making that hard earned money on the sale of those cattle had been very important for him and his new family. He was curious and disappointed at Mike's strange indifference. But he was a man now, a husband and a father, responsible for making his own way in the world.

He explained to Johanna that they would have to save as much money as possible to pay down on another place. Even with saving for two years, they would have to get a mortgage from a bank. Ranching was all he knew and all he wanted to do, so he needed a good amount of land for grazing, provided it ever rained. There had still been little or no rain for several years. At least he hadn't taken all of his cattle to Dodge City, and had enough to keep going.

"Didn't your father look at a good place a few years back?" B.G. asked.

"Yes, it has a house and water well. It also has a pecan orchard and a small peach orchard. There must have been thousands of buckets of water hauled to those trees," Johanna replied. B.G. shook his head from side to side in frustration. "And now he wants a motorcar!"

B.G. would need to talk to Guenther about Mr. Fields. Hopefully, Guenther still had the information.

Johanna knew where that old farm was. Her father had described it to her in great detail. She remembered that he told her the house needed a lot of work, but they could do it, and she knew he would help with the repairs. They would have to wait to do anything more than just what was necessary, but it would be livable. It already had a good well, which was something they couldn't do without, even for one day. Johanna hoped the place was still available and that they could move right away. There would be more room for a family there, too. She didn't want to live on Mike's ranch anymore. Neither of them understood Mike's actions, but he had hurt her husband, and that wasn't acceptable to Johanna.

She would speak with her father about the money. She knew her father's funds were limited and tied up in the shop, but he could probably help. B.G. wouldn't want her to talk to Guenther or even think of borrowing money from him. But that piece of land, if it was still available, backed up to Sandy Creek. If they were going to have to move, they'd never find a better place than that one.

Johanna had been planning a trip to the hotel and general store. Sara hadn't seen Joseph since the day he was born. Abel Cain, Luke Matthews, nor any of their other friends had seen him, either. It was time for Baby Joe to meet everyone. Now was a good time to go. It would be a good opportunity to find out more about that piece of land and house that might possibly be their new home, a perfect place for baby Joe to grow up.

As she changed and dressed the baby, she cooed, "Baby Joe, it is time for you to meet my friends. We need to talk to Grandpa about a bigger house for us to live in."

Chapter Thirty-eight

Johanna sat in the shade of the pecan trees watching Joseph play on a quilt, while Baby Sara Elizabeth lay beside her. She was very content that day, kicking her feet and reaching for the clouds with her little hands. They had come out to watch B.G. thrash the pecan trees. Johanna had packed a picnic lunch to share with B.G., when he could finally take a break to eat a bit. She also brought enough food for the hired hand.

The pecan orchard wasn't large, only about twenty trees or so, but it was far too big a job for one person to complete in a timely manner. Once the pecans were on the ground, they had to be picked up right away, lest the wildlife get them first. Caring for the fruit trees, the pecan trees and the garden were tasks that Johanna usually managed with B.G.'s help, but her difficult pregnancy and caring for a baby and for Joseph interfered with that and most everything else she tried to do or wanted to do. She had her hands full with those two. Joseph was at a curious age, into everything, and she had to watch him closely all day every day. He was big enough to open the door by himself and get outside before she could catch him. Chasing after him sometimes meant running outside to catch him. Although Sara Elizabeth wasn't crawling yet, she wasn't well, so Johanna was reluctant to leave her alone, even for a minute.

The hired hand was a new fellow, David, who had come to Texas from Arkansas, looking for permanent work. He would take any kind of work to hold him over. B.G. didn't expect he would stay around very long. However long he chose to stay, B.G. was grateful to have his help. There was no one else around to hire right now. He was a good hand and smart. It always made Johanna wonder what brought someone all the way to the Hill Country, alone and with no apparent ambition. David didn't even have a good horse, just a stubborn old mule. The Cain's had hired him do a few odd jobs at the hotel, as well.

Having cattle to manage, B.G. didn't have a lot of time for extra chores like pecans or peaches or a garden, but he had to do all of Johanna's chores and manage the cattle, too.

Baby Sara Elizabeth had been sick ever since she was born. Johanna had the same problem with her milk as she'd had with Joseph. Even the goat's milk didn't seem to agree with this baby, though. She had diarrhea all the time and cried endlessly. Unable to hire help, they both just managed as best they could. Johanna felt badly for the baby. It was sad that sweet baby was sick so much of the time. Seeing her smile and cry at the same time sometimes broke her mother's heart.

Sara Cain came by often, but she still had her hands full with the hotel and general store. Both Sara and Etta helped out whenever possible. Etta frequently brought leftovers from the cafe. That was always a delight, as she usually brought some of her magical pie for dessert.

B.G. was hoping pecan prices would be good this year; at least better than the cattle prices had been. He hardly made anything on his cattle at the last sale. Most prices on everything were down, and transportation prices were up. The railroads and suppliers were scalping the farmers and ranchers. Something would have to change soon.

Drought was taking its toll. Rain seemed to be avoiding Texas with a vengeance. B.G. couldn't remember the last time there was a good rain. He was fearful that his pastures were going to be over-grazed. Finding some land to rent or lease and moving the cattle wouldn't be easy. It meant having to herd them somewhere, which was a lot of work to go a short distance. For those same reasons, many of the ranchers were selling off their herds for slaughter. B.G. was trying to avoid buying feed and resist selling at such low prices, but the options were running out. The last thing he wanted to do was sell his good cattle for slaughter too soon. He'd already lost enough money on cattle after that drive to Dodge City for Mike.

The air started to cool as the breeze began to shift out of the north. Johanna gathered the babies and walked the short distance to their home. Young Joseph helped his mom carry the basket. He was tired and ready for a much-needed nap. Baby Sara Elizabeth was still quiet, and although she wriggled and squirmed as usual, she was the most content she had ever been. Johanna put them both down for a nap and lay down herself.

It was after dark when B.G. came home. Johanna awakened when she heard him enter the house. They both quickly went to waken the babies from too long a nap. The sunshine and the afternoon outing had put all three of them in a deep restful sleep.

Joseph sleepily rubbed his eyes and sat up in his bed, while his dad patted his back and tousled his hair.

A frantic, guttural scream came from the other side of the darkened room. Holding her baby in outstretched hands, Johanna screamed, "Do something, do something, she isn't breathing, do something!"

B.G. took the baby, but she was dark and her thin little body was cool. Baby Sara Elizabeth had given up her struggle. On the day that Johanna thought the baby was actually better, her little life passed peacefully, quietly away. Johanna was filled with anguish at the passing of her baby alone in her crib, rather than in her mother's arms. "If only I hadn't fallen asleep," Johanna cried.

A funeral for a baby was pretty hard on that gathering of very close families and friends. Luke Matthews performed the service; as always there when he was needed. Sara Elizabeth Steven was buried beside her grandpa Guenther, there in the little cemetery nestled beside Sandy Creek and the road to the crossing bridge.

B.G. and Johanna held Joseph close and went home to face the empty crib. Johanna sobbed for days. It was all she could do to take care of Joseph, mechanically going through the motions of her daily routine.

A broken heart, unable to eat, vomiting what she did manage to eat, unable to sleep, Johanna was inconsolable. The stress on her body and her unborn baby was too much. The cramping started in the middle of night and got worse with each hour. Johanna recognized the pain, and knew it was too soon. It was much too soon.

Chapter Thirty-nine

There were no sidewalks, no streets, no utilities and no clean water. There was no city government and little or no law enforcement. There were over twenty thousand people living in tents, but that number had already begun to diminish, as many of the would-be homesteaders had failed in their efforts to become property owners. Discouraged, some settlers were already leaving to return to their home states, in spite of the rapid progress being made each day, establishing the city. For those who remained, the boom continued and others came to replace those who left. The building of Lawton, Oklahoma went forward in spite of the many obstacles and challenges.

Dodge and Cheri had completed their building and were awaiting the arrival of all the furnishings, stock and supplies they'd ordered. They continued to stay in the wagon until furniture arrived. It was comfortable and dry, unlike the conditions in the tents.

The red dust that constantly floated and swirled above the ground coated everything in sight. All of the activity in the town made it even worse. The workmen wore rags tied around their noses and mouths to help them breathe; their faces were streaked with red-stained sweat.

Then the skies decided to open over Lawton, and it rained for weeks. Wagons bogged down in the thick red mud. Long planks, used for makeshift bridges or sidewalks, lay over giant puddles in the streets to help people navigate from one place to another. Little did they know that unusual period of moisture on the plains would return to normal conditions, then drought. In just a few short years, they would wish for that rain.

Cheri was amazed and grateful for Dodge's abilities. It seemed to her that he had done this many times before. In fact, he had done it at least once before, along with Abel and Sara Cain.

Dodge was quick to recognize that there were skilled people available in need of money and work. He posted a sign on their empty lot offering employment. A line formed before he finished staking it in the ground. The very first hire had a wagon and immediately began hauling the lumber to start their building.

Together, Dodge and Cheri looked through catalogs, talked to the many drummers and craftsmen who filled the town, and ordered the furnishings and supplies to stock the store. Cheri spent hours cleaning away the endless red dust and mud and planning the layout of the shelves and cabinets that would furnish the store and the home upstairs. She looked at fashion and ladies' magazines that offered advice and direction on homemaking. She had no idea what it took to make a home, but wanted to be sure to stock the items ladies would be seeking.

Cheri often daydreamed about her and Dodge living upstairs together. She even went so far as to imagine that they might one day marry. She had decided that she loved him and felt certain he felt the same, although he'd never said so. Their nights together were certainly better and different than any she had ever spent with a man. She had never known the gentle tenderness, the ardent kisses that aroused her so. They lived in the wagon together and she hoped they would continue to live together above the store.

Each day when the supply wagons rolled into town, everyone ran to see what might have arrived, Cheri among them. The first to arrive for the millinery department at the store was a beautiful rounded glass front display cabinet, perfect for gloves, scarves, feathers and pins. Cheri was elated. Dodge couldn't keep from being amused at her excitement. He was more interested in checking the cabinet for damage, of which he was pleased to find none.

Aside from a few other cabinets and a decorative counter top, the store and millinery shop were almost complete. Once it all finally began coming, more and more stock arrived each day. Much like the Cain's General Store, there was everything except food in the new store.

Dodge had worked hard on the building and the store and on teaching Cheri the things she needed to know, and he was proud and pleased at the way she quickly understood each task and took it over herself.

The home upstairs was almost complete. They moved the contents from the wagon after the bed finally arrived. The kitchen and bathroom were downstairs and both had the newest most modern appliances. Dodge had installed indoor plumbing, but it was downstairs.

To Cheri's disappointment, Dodge announced he would not be moving into her home upstairs. His explanation was that a lady of stature, a shop owner and merchant, wouldn't live with a man out of wedlock, nor should she reveal her past, no matter the circumstances. She should command the respect of the ladies of Lawton, those ladies who would be her potential customers, or not.

Come they did. The ladies of Lawton, tired of red dust and mud and living in tents, patiently waiting for homes to be completed, were eager for a pleasant distraction. They slowly began to visit the newest store to open its doors, with its glass door and chairs and potted plants on the walkway. Splendid it was, with display windows full of exciting fashion hats and accessories, now open for business.

MISS CHERI'S

MILLINERY SHOP & HOME GOODS

Chapter Forty

The few headstones in the little cemetery were lined up in a row along a makeshift fence across the back. One of Mike Terrell's ranch hands had built a nice gate a long time ago. It was close to the bridge that crossed over Sandy Creek. Two tall, leaning cypress trees cast an afternoon shadow over a large, flat granite stone. It created a peaceful place to sit and reflect.

Johanna sat on the big stone while Joseph climbed on the fence and swung on the gate. She had come to see the headstone that B.G. had set for baby Sara Elizabeth's marker. Recovering from the miscarriage had taken awhile, so it was her first trip back to the cemetery. The little family had dwindled to three members again, after Sara Elizabeth's death and the miscarriage.

Johanna knew most of the people who were buried there, Etta's husband, Daniel, Baby Sara Elizabeth, and her grandfather, Guenther, who had been laid to rest there shortly after Joseph was born. There was a Civil War soldier buried there. She decided his family must have moved on a long time ago. If he had a family or if they had ever been there, she'd never known of them. There were also two five-year-old twin boys, who mysteriously died on the same day. Curious about what awful fate they met, she didn't know of that family, either. *Poor little fellows,* she thought.

Johanna remembered when her father went missing for several days and the night B.G. and Luke Matthews finally found him.

No one would ever really know what happened. The last time Sara saw him he was standing in the doorway of the hotel kitchen having a cup of coffee. He was leaving early that morning for a trip to the telegraph office, then planned to travel back by way of Johanna's home, for a visit with his grandson.

Guenther was the happiest he had been in years and so proud to be a grandpa. Joseph would be told many stories about his grandpa. Johanna had begun a journal when she and her father set out on their journey to Texas. Someday, Joseph would be able to read all about it and know about his family.

It saddened Johanna to remember that morning. Once it was finally discovered that Guenther hadn't returned to the shop or to the hotel for more than a day, B.G. and Luke Matthews went out to search for him. They were gone all afternoon and into the night, finally finding him on the old ranch road out beyond Johanna and B.G.'s house. They came up on the wreckage in the moonlight, but it was too dark to see very well. It took a while before they located him. They carried a lantern and were searching around through the brush when they finally came upon his body, confirming their fears. It looked as though he tried to crawl off the road and under a tree for some protection, where he finally died. There was no doctor available to determine the actual cause of his death, but he had a severe head wound, to which they attributed the cause.

Daylight the next morning brought a large group of people to look at the wreckage. It appeared that something must have spooked the horses and that they had run the wagon up on a boulder causing it to overturn. The harnesses were detached and the end of the tongue was broken into two pieces. *If I had only been at home,* Johanna sighed; t*hat was the day I went in to town to talk to him about the house and to visit Sara. If only I'd been at home.*

Almost as sad and devastating to Johanna was that Pebble had to be destroyed, too. Both of his front legs were broken. He was suffering. Pebble had been Johanna's friend and companion and connection to her mother. Many of the memories of her mother were of times shared with him. After Johanna had calmed down a bit, B.G. took his rifle and went back out to the wreckage. As he squeezed the trigger, he softly spoke to Pebble, "I'm sorry, boy."

David helped B.G. take him out back of the orchard and bury him there. B.G. made a marker with his name on it.

Now they are all gone. If not for B.G. and Joseph, I would have no one, Johanna sighed.

Johanna hadn't known about her father's final plan to sell the blacksmith shop until Sara shared her last conversation with Guenther about the bulletins at the telegraph offices. Johanna knew it was a bulletin at a telegraph office that had brought them to Texas.

There was never a single inquiry or response to any of the bulletins that Guenther posted. No one was interested in a blacksmith shop in the Hill Country. Eventually, B.G. sold off most of the equipment and kept the rest. The doors to the shop were closed and locked. The Terrell ranch didn't even exist anymore, so there was no need for a blacksmith there, either. The community couldn't support a blacksmith. Eventually, B.G. boarded up the windows and doors to keep vermin from making it their home.

As Johanna prepared to leave the cemetery, she knelt with her hand resting upon Sara Elizabeth's little marker. "My sweet angel, Mother is here, I love you. I love you. I'm so sorry. I will always love you; never, never forget you!"

At the end of that emotional day, Johanna clung to her husband. B.G. loved and needed his wife as much as she loved and needed him. He had held his home and family together while Johanna's heart and body healed. It had been a long time coming. He hadn't allowed himself to grieve until that night. The tears finally came.

Surrounded by their love and comfort to each other, their tears flamed into the passion that had always burned between them.

Chapter Forty-one

"Mr. Terrell, Mr. Terrell, can you hear me, sir? Do you want to move to your bed, now?"

Mike's nurse had to clean up all the mess and bathe him before she could help him to his bed. His stroke had left him unable to make sense with his speech. He was unable to walk, nor control his bodily functions. The little he could do was blurt out curse words and show his distaste for those who were employed to help him.

Mike's dream of living in the hotel in Austin and driving around town in his new motorcar hadn't quite come true. It was finally discovered that the strange behavior he'd exhibited was the result of a series of strokes and senility. No one, especially Mike, was aware that they were occurring until he had the worst one, the one that nearly killed him. His survival was not a good thing. Incapable of caring for himself and unable to communicate, he lived in a near silent world of frustration and helplessness.

The arrangements that Mike had previously made, to live at the hotel, were still in place. He was moved into his suite when he was well enough to do so. His caregivers attended him there. Most of his days were spent sitting on the balcony in the sunshine. He did seem to enjoy watching the hustle and bustle of life in the city. Fortunately, blessed sleep filled the rest of his time.

Although his plans to transfer the ranch prior to his death had been performed under the influence of mild senility, it had been the best thing that could have happened for him. The same applied to his care. Mike could live the rest of his days, such as they were, in the comfort of a luxurious hotel, with plenty of people to care for him.

The drummer who had ordered Mike's motorcar heard the news of Mike's illness long before the motorcar was ever delivered. Sara and Abel agreed to purchase the motorcar when it arrived. It was clear that Mike would never be able to drive it. Sara was always ready to step into the future. Learning to drive and having a motorcar would save a lot of time traveling into Austin for supplies and such. It would be helpful in many ways. The drummer agreed to teach both Sara and Abel how to drive.

In a short amount of time, many other people in Texas had motorcars, especially the wealthy, and frequently the doctors, who made good use of them and were some of the few who were able to afford them.

No one ever comes to see me. Sara C-C-C-, damn, what's her name, she comes more than B.G. comes. Ungrateful bastard! After all I did for him. B.G. never comes to see me. They need to come take me out of this damn sun, Mike's thoughts raced, as he was more agitated than usual that day.

B.G. tried to visit Mike as often as possible, but he had a home, family, and herd to manage. He'd also lost a child and his wife wasn't well. He didn't have a whole day to spare. He couldn't really talk to Mike when he went and wasn't sure whether Mike understood that he came.

Mike was in good hands, so his welfare was on the bottom of B.G.'s list of responsibilities. He loved Mike, but the events he had set in motion dealt a blow to B.G. and his family, one that did not change their lives for the better.

Chapter Forty-two

Eli Ayers and his group of investors, merchants and tradesmen boarded the train in Memphis. They would travel to St. Louis, then on as far as the tracks had been laid toward Lawton, Oklahoma. It was designated to be the county seat of Comanche County, and was near Fort Sill, just a few hours to the north. It was the intention of the group to bid on the town lots that were being made available through a public auction. The guide service had arranged for wagons, supplies and horses to be awaiting their arrival at the end of the rail line. From there, they would set out for Lawton. Within months of the establishment of Lawton as the county seat, the railroad had expanded all the way in to Lawton, which was joined shortly by the railroad from California.

The business of providing guide service had changed over the years. Unless a group was bound to a destination far out West, they were usually headed to and through already settled areas with established roads and trails. But his service provided a degree of security and convenience for those who were not inclined to handle the challenges of the journey or the frontier. Having someone to make all the arrangements and literally be delivered to their destination appealed to many, especially those with financial means.

Just after the onset of their trip, Eli had received word that there was a huge tent city with thousands of people already at the site. He began preparing for the objections and complaints that would be coming from his group. He was grateful there were no women in the group, as they would be an added amount of trouble and their comfort would have to be a concern. Just thinking about the crowd of land-hungry opportunists made him rethink staying more than a couple of days.

Unable to predict such an outpouring of homesteaders seeking town sites, he was already changing his plans of returning on horseback alone. There would no doubt be many in his group who would be returning to Memphis. Anyone who won a lot would need to be prepared to stay in order to protect his interests. However, Eli knew the likelihood of winning a lot would be small.

Returning with a group, especially a disgruntled group, was not something Eli looked forward to or planned. It would be the first time ever for him to escort anyone back to Memphis, rather than from Memphis.

The rumors had been correct. The approach to Lawton revealed a cloud of red dust that could be seen for miles and miles away. There were many, many people and much activity packed in to those few square miles. Red-stained white tents lined imaginary streets, and campfires burned, adding smoke to the already dusty air. Many of the people were wearing bandanas around their faces to filter the air they breathed.

The rumblings among the group had already begun. Always well equipped, Eli began distributing tents and helping set them up. Contrary to the desires of the group, each tent would have four cots, and would have to serve four gentlemen. There were no other accommodations available, although there would be very soon.

Eli hadn't set out to bid on town lots, but decided he could sell it if he won one. So, when the time came, his name went into the till, along with all the others. He had begun to consider staying in Oklahoma.

He liked everything about Oklahoma. Opportunities abounded; railroads, mines, farming, law enforcement. He liked the climate and even liked the sticky red dust and the frequent dust storms that kicked up out of nowhere.

The auction came and went. Eli didn't win a lot, nor did any of his group, save for one gentleman. That one and only gentleman, accompanied by a representative, was also the only one who would have been prepared to stay. He was the only member of the group to bring along a representative who could remain at the site to protect his interests. Eli felt it was a fair accomplishment and deserved by the gentleman for good planning. He had undoubtedly read the newspaper accounts of squatters taking other's claims as soon as they left to go file the legal claim.

Arrangements were made for the others to return. As for himself, he would escort them to the train, stay long enough to sell the wagons and horses, then return to Lawton. He had finally decided he had found his permanent home.

Eli knew there would be plenty of work available for a man willing to work. In fact, he did find work right away. A man named Dodge Blackburn, who had won a lot, staked a "Help Wanted" sign right in the middle of his lot. Eli accepted a job and immediately took his wagon to pick up lumber. Blackburn and his companion had plans for a two-story building.

Eli was not only smitten with this new burgeoning town, but Dodge's companion Cheri intrigued him as well.

Chapter Forty-three

From the first day it opened, the store was busy. A stream of customers came in daily and it was almost impossible to keep the shelves stocked. Cheri and Dodge were constantly ordering more. Many customers returned for the second and third time. Stock flew off the shelves. It was surprising the number of people who came to Lawton without adequate supplies or equipment. The store carried only household items, but people had come without those items, too.

The millinery shop wasn't as busy, but after all, there was no place to wear finery. The dusty streets of Lawton would soon be covered over and paved, however. There were a few churches under construction. The trend would change soon.

Meanwhile, Cheri had plenty of opportunity to learn the business and had done so. She was comfortable with the ladies of Lawton. Her confidence had soared. Dodge had shown her how to manage the accounting and the banking. They'd opened an account at the first bank to open its doors. She had learned how to make the deposit and pay the bills. She knew how to order the stock and to check it off the order slip and invoice and against the totals when it arrived.

Cheri would often stop whatever she was doing and look around the store, up the staircase to the decorative windows, run her hand along the counter top, open and close the glass doors on the cabinets, and wonder at the life she had now. Each morning when she woke up, she lay in her beautiful fluffy bed and rubbed her eyes to make certain it wasn't a dream.

"I love you, Dodge Blackburn." She caught herself after saying that out loud. She had finally realized Dodge wasn't going to marry her. She knew he loved her, but not the marrying type of love. She was grateful for any love he had for her; she missed him in her bed, missed his kisses and the warmth of his strong body against her. She knew he would never come to her again. Cheri's experiences had been with men wanting her, not her wanting them, like she wanted Dodge. He was the only man she'd ever wanted, the only one with whom…

More stores were opening their doors. Many businesses and homes had been completed and families had joined their husbands and fathers after months, even years of waiting. In a short time, Lawton had begun to bustle with real purpose, becoming a real city with sidewalks, streets and utilities. A school had finally opened its doors to students.

Cheri was an important part of it all. She had been there from the beginning. The town folks actually asked her opinions, and invited her to join their organizations and to come into their homes.

Dodge could see that his work was done. Not only had Cheri left her old life, she had embraced the new one. She was a successful, respected merchant in the city of Lawton. She had developed friends and people who cared about her. Yes, his work was done.

Has it really been seven years, or more, since I last saw Sara and Abel? Dodge wondered. He really couldn't remember. It might have been more. He thought about it a minute and decided it had been a lot longer than he'd imagined. It was time he gathered the courage to go see Sara. Truth was, being away from Sara was much easier than being near her. He decided to put it off a little longer because he knew that once he went back, he wouldn't be able to leave again, not that he had ever intended to leave to begin with. But there was one more thing he wanted to do before he returned to Sandy Creek. He wanted to see California. He had heard many stories about California. *Maybe I'll try my hand at panning for gold,* he chuckled.

He had never sent Sara an address, nor had he written to her again after that one letter. *If I'm going to leave for California there is no reason to send her an address now,* he pondered. But he would write to her. He owed her that. He was ashamed that he hadn't been better at writing to her, letting her know what was happening and that he was still alive.

He wasn't the same person as when he left. A lot had happened. To his knowledge, Sara knew nothing about any of it, not about Cheri, or even that Cheri existed. She didn't know about west Texas, the lost saddlebags, killing the Indians, the store in Lawton. Nothing. *How can I explain all that in a letter?*

Although he was curious and concerned about Sara and Abel and the hotel and general store, it would have to wait.

The train could take him all the way to California. He would leave Little Bit with Cheri and buy a horse when he got there. Little Bit was getting pretty old. It was time for him to rest.

He'd heard there were trolley cars in San Francisco, and ships that docked there from the Orient, from all over the world. He would be able to smell the salt air again and wander the docks like he'd done as a child in Galveston.

It would be very hard to tell Cheri, but he would. He wouldn't leave without saying goodbye.

She was standing behind the counter, closing out the register for the day. She looked up as he entered. That same beautiful smile spread across her face as she greeted him. That same familiar feeling warmed him deep inside.

He knew she was totally his for the taking, but it would be so wrong.

Chapter Forty-four

Most of the rocks on one side of the cistern had fallen away as the mortar crumbled from between them. Sara suspected there might be more to that story. Something caused those rocks to fall, but no one seemed to know anything about it. The repairs had to be done, just the same.

She gazed out the window of the hotel kitchen and watched David and Abel toil with the effort, neither of them familiar with rock and mortar. It brought a smile to her face.

David had come along just when they really needed the help. She and Abel couldn't manage without David and Etta. David wouldn't be there long. As soon as he could find permanent work, he would leave. Age had caught up with Etta, and she was hardly the help Sara really needed anymore. After Daniel died, it seemed Etta lost a lot of her spunk.

Dodge and Johanna were truly missed. It appeared Dodge would never return. Johanna had her life with B.G.

Steven. They seemed happy enough, but losing the babies had changed them. She suspected Johanna might be pregnant again.

Sara enjoyed driving her motorcar. She made frequent trips to Austin, at least once a month. She could go, make all the stops for supplies, bank deposits and so on, and return in one day. She always took time to go see Mike, even if she wasn't sure whether he knew she was there.

Mike Terrell's influence in their little community and the lives of all those people would never be forgotten, as far as Sara was concerned. She remembered the fall festivals that were held each year, how Mike and his hands would come storming up on their horses and the wonderful barbecue his ranch hands cooked, a familiar annual ritual. She missed the festivals, but there were too few people or families there to participate, and too little interest anymore. Mike wasn't there either, so there was no steer to barbecue and no ranch hands to cook it, and no cowhands to storm up on their horses. For that matter, there were too fewer people to bring the rest of the food, or make it fun.

It is odd how this has happened, one family after another has left, then Guenther died and the blacksmith shop closed. The Terrell ranch and Mike, and all his ranch hands are gone now. It was hardly noticeable at first, one person or family at a time. Today, I look around and there is no one here anymore, except us. Even a lot of the farms have sold and no one lives on them, to come in here. Sara sighed, and went on about her chores. There was a lot to do before she left for Austin that day.

The road to Austin would take her by the ranch, which belonged to the university now, or she could take the cutoff and it could take her through where the encampment used to be. The clearing was still plainly there, but had begun to cover over with vines and weeds. Of the people who had lived there and had come and gone, Sara wondered why they never attempted to make their permanent homes there, rather than always leaving for other places. *Even Dodge has left and never returned.* Just one letter; she'd received only one letter, and she hadn't heard from him again. Sara's heart ached for Dodge, the closest thing she had to family. *Please be okay. Please write to me. Please come back, Dodge.*

Sara's thoughts were interrupted when the bell at the hotel desk rang. That bell rang so seldom anymore. *Could we possibly have a guest, or just another curious passer-by?* It was too early in the day for a guest. The few guests that stopped and stayed the night were people who'd found themselves too far from Austin to make it before nightfall. She missed the days when someone actually came to stay awhile.

Sara knew the inevitable had happened. When the railroad didn't come through, the community couldn't thrive. Businesses, even farmers and ranchers, took their crops, livestock and business nearer to the railroad stop. The little bit of commerce that had developed disappeared. Business at the Cain Hotel and General Store was almost non-existent. Things had changed in just those few years.

It seems the cycle of life, either for people or a place, takes care of itself. Our business is falling off and we can't manage it anymore, even if it weren't. Sara's melancholy thoughts followed her as she hurried to the desk.

To her surprise it was the drummer, from whom they'd purchased the motorcar, and from whom they'd learned to drive. He hadn't stopped by in a long time. Sara was happy to see him. He traveled around the state all the time and always had news.

Over a cup of coffee, the drummer shared information about laws that were being considered pertaining to roads, motorcar ownership, and licenses that were going to be required and taxes. There was even talk about the creation of a state department to manage the roads and highways, rather than it being done by volunteers or managed by the counties. They discussed the upcoming elections and cotton prices, which were both the biggest topics he was hearing about from the farmers and merchants. The other major topic of the day was the toll the drought was taking on everything, especially the farmers and cattle ranchers. The drummer had lots of news, about which Sara was eager to hear.

With so few people or visitors coming through, they were isolated from news of current events that those visitors often brought with them. The newspaper from Austin seldom covered the local issues and concerns of other small towns and communities.

Although Sara knew that the hotel and store would probably never sell, she had also finally accepted that it was time to at least try to sell it or close the doors. It was time to accept that the opportunities for the success of their business and the community had come and gone. It was time for her and Abel to move to one of the towns nearby, or to Austin, before they were too old to take on that huge task or start another enterprise. *Maybe we could move back to Galveston*, she considered. The idea of listening to the surf and the gulls for the rest of her life appealed to her. After all this time, after all that had happened, that her parents didn't live to join her in the Hill Country, that she and Abel had to accept there would be no children, maybe she should consider returning home. *It is an exciting, yet tranquil, place to be.* Going home to Galveston appealed to her.

Chapter Forty-five

Johanna watched B.G. walk toward the barn. His long strides closed that distance quickly. Although silver streaks peppered his hair, he was still a handsome man. Even after all these years he still took her breath away. Twirling around the dance floor at the fall festival seemed like yesterday. It was just daybreak and he had work to do and a long day ahead of him. His shadow, Joseph, followed him wherever he went. Joseph worked hard, right along beside his dad, every day.

B.G. was moving some of his herd to a neighbor's pasture. David was coming out to help him for a while. His neighbor had sold off most of his herd and was willing to let B.G. use the pasture for a small payment. Many ranchers and farmers were selling off their stock. Feed prices were high and lack of rain meant there was little grass left for grazing. He had tried alternating the pastures, but it didn't help much. B.G. hoped to avoid buying feed if he could make use of someone else's pastures. The bigger problem was getting the cattle to the other pastures. It usually meant taking down fence, which was a lot of work for one man. Having David around was a blessing, while it lasted.

Johanna hadn't the heart to tell B.G. that her flow hadn't come for several months. She had hoped that she was past the childbearing years. The miscarriages and infant deaths she had experienced over the years had taken a toll on her body and spirit, leaving her unable to help as much as needed.

It hurt to watch her husband struggle. She wished their lives had been different. She wondered if B.G. still loved her.

Joseph would start to school again in the fall. The distance to the schoolhouse was too great a distance for him to walk, now, since the school moved. Either she or his father would have to take him to school. Maybe there would be some other children taking a wagon to school and he could ride along with them. She'd kept him home too long as it was. She watched him follow his dad, trying to keep up. He had grown a lot over the summer and his giant steps made his ankle short pants look even shorter. "I need to make that boy some pants," she said out loud.

Johanna met the new pregnancy with much concern and dread. The births were just so difficult and painful. She couldn't bear the thought of losing another baby.

So far, she was feeling better than usual, but didn't want to get her hopes up.

The fragrance of cooked peaches filled the kitchen. Johanna was canning peaches and grape juice. She had managed to sell a lot of the peaches when they were fresh picked. That money was much needed and would be put to good use in the household. The remaining peaches were canned before they spoiled. Joseph and his dad loved the peaches best cooked in a pie or cobbler.

A trip to the countryside produced bushels of mustang grapes. Such a sour fruit on the vine, they made the best juice and jelly. The grapes grew wild along the fences or tree line and along the roads throughout the area. Usually several of the wives in the area would join together for a trip to pick grapes, and sometimes dewberries. The dewberries always made a good cobbler or pie when they were in season.

Johanna's garden had produced big bright red to-matoes and an abundance of other vegetables. Hauling water from the creek, day in and day out, had been much more successful than she ever expected. Canned tomatoes, green beans, pickles, jelly and juice lined the shelves in the shed, evidence of her work. Johanna had watched her mother canning, but hadn't really learned how until Etta pulled her into the kitchen and showed her how it was done. She could make a pretty good peach pie, too, but hadn't mastered Etta's talent, which was baking the best pies anyone had ever tasted! Johanna secretly, lovingly suspected that Etta cast a voodoo spell over her pies and food. Those who ate her cooking were smitten for life. Born of slaves, Etta still had some peculiar behavior and phrases she quietly spoke to herself or sang at times.

Johanna roused from her daydreaming to watch B.G. and David, along with Joseph, ride out of sight. She knew they wouldn't be back until after dark, tired and hungry.

She decided a fried chicken would be a good supper for her hungry men, and went out to the coop to fetch one.

Chapter Forty-six

After completing the work on the millinery shop and home goods store for Dodge Blackburn, Eli Ayers moved on to become a successful contractor in Lawton. Oil had been discovered in the territory and there was talk about statehood. There were already folks who'd discovered that Oklahoma was not meant for them. They were leaving for other areas or going back home. Some couldn't live with the dust and sticky red clay. Once the natural grasses were removed, the soil was loose and wouldn't hold. The dust was even worse than before, and any little bit of rain produced big washouts.

He was surprised to learn Dodge Blackburn had left for California. Blackburn's associate, Cheri, was running the store alone, with the exception of a few employees. He thought they were man and wife at first, but had since learned that was not the case. Cheri was not married and had never been. She was a very attractive young wom-

211

an and had caught the eye of several gentlemen in Lawton, including Eli himself.

Eli had only ever had an interest in one other young woman, Johanna Gurganis, a girl who now lived in Texas, and from whom he had stolen a last minute kiss the very last time he saw her. He had thought of her often, but had never heard from that family again. He imagined that she was probably married and had a family by now. *One thing for certain, whoever married her is a lucky man.*

Eli didn't have a legitimate reason to go to the home goods store or the millinery store. He didn't have a home; rather he lived in his wagon. He had no use for gloves or ladies hats, as he had no wife.

There was a camping area set aside for the many workmen who were there. Eli lived among them. They had come from all over the country to help build Lawton. Many would eventually stay and make Lawton their permanent home, just as he had. Many would leave and move on to another job or another state.

Miss Cheri's Millinery and Home Goods Store did not sell food, but on occasion Cheri would allow someone to leave a basket of tomatoes or squash or corn out on the walkway. Eli noticed a basket of potatoes there and decided to take advantage of the opportunity. He gathered a few potatoes and entered the store. Just as he did so, someone came running out the door, bumping into him and knocking him to the floor. Cheri was screaming, "Stop him, stop him, he has stolen our money!" Just then a bullet whizzed by Eli's head as he looked up and saw Cheri aiming a gun at the thief. Eli jumped up, ran after the thief and tackled him as he was trying to mount his horse. He pulled him off the horse, knocked him to the ground, and sat on him until help came. The sheriff came running when he heard all the commotion.

Eli could see that Cheri was shaken, but relieved and grateful for his help. "He would have gotten away, if not for you," she insisted. Then she stopped and looked at Eli closely. "Aren't you one of the men who helped Dodge build our store? Come inside." It was the end of the day. Cheri had been counting the money and preparing the deposit when the thief ran up to the counter and grabbed it. She was aggravated with herself for not noticing such a character in the store, especially someone who obviously had no real purpose in there.

Cheri invited Eli upstairs to her home to share a drink and a toast to express her appreciation. "How can I possibly repay you? The thief almost got away with all of our money."

Eli, who was considering himself lucky to still be alive after nearly being shot, seized this opportunity to ask if he could call on her again, officially. Cheri graciously accepted.

Cheri had been lonely in Dodge's absence. She also knew there would be no future with him. It was time she opened herself to other gentlemen callers. She found Eli to be very handsome, and was looking forward to his visit. As much as she wished that her last moments with Dodge could mean something, she knew she had to let him go. She doubted that he would ever return to Lawton, even though he promised he would. Either way, she knew there was no future with Dodge.

Cheri imagined that if Dodge ever came back from California, he would go to Texas. He would head for the Cain Hotel and General Store and his lovely Sara. *I can't compete with a lifetime of love for someone else.* Cheri remembered how Dodge would often call her Sara, especially when he had drunk too much and came to visit their wagon for the evening, back at the encampment. *Gosh, that seems like a lifetime ago!*

ଚଠଓଷ

Cheri was working in the store when she felt her head begin to spin and she was gripped with nausea. She grasped the counter to keep from falling, but she lost consciousness and dropped to the floor. A cool wet cloth, applied to her face by an employee, roused her. Suddenly, she felt fine, and was on her feet brushing herself off, trying to brush off her embarrassment, too. Her upset stomach and dizziness had passed again. *Oh my, what is wrong with me lately? Oh!* Instinctively, she knew exactly what was wrong. Her mind began to search for a solution.

When Dodge built the store, he had made an entrance to Cheri's home at the top of a stairway on the outside of the structure. There was a small private porch and doorway. She could enter her home from inside or outside. Eli appeared at the outside door at exactly 6:30 p.m., right on time. Cheri prepared their dinner. Their evening was short and very cordial. Cheri wanted to make the best impression possible. When the evening came to a close, Eli lingered at the door. She stood close to him. When he leaned to kiss her lightly, she responded with her mouth open a bit, hesitating to pull her lips away. She withdrew, dropping her eyes, as if embarrassed. Virile man that he was, he pulled her to him firmly and kissed her hungrily. Cheri pulled away, "Oh, we mustn't. Good night, Mr. Ayers."

He stopped by the store several more times before Cheri reluctantly agreed to allow him to call on her again.

On the night of that visit, Cheri was the one who was surprised, as she did not expect this rugged frontiersman to be such a forceful, yet tender, lover. She already had a fondness for Eli and knew she could learn to love him. If nothing else, her bed would be warm.

Later, when Cheri finally told Eli that he was going to be a father, he took her to a preacher, right then and there. She didn't feel good about deceiving him, but had no alternative. The ladies of Lawton would never accept such an abomination, an unmarried woman in the family way. They would shun her and the store. It would destroy the store. She made a silent promise to be the best wife Eli could ever hope for.

When a letter finally arrived from Dodge, and she had his address in hand, Cheri wrote to him explaining about Eli Ayers and their marriage. When the child was born, she wrote to him once again to share the good news about his namesake. It was her decision that if Dodge ever returned, she would tell him the whole story; otherwise, no one would ever know.

Chapter Forty-seven

The salty spray peppered his face as the boat repeatedly rose up and over the swells, then plunged deep between the waves. He stood at the bow, watching the seagulls fly in circles above, each hoping for an opportunity to pluck a meal from one of the many nets, which were thrown and gathered and emptied onto the boat. Often, a brave gull would boldly swoop down to grab a fish right off the deck. Dodge had taken a job on a fishing boat, the closest he could possibly get to the sea.

The train from Lawton had taken him across the plains, up through the Sierra Nevada and out to San Francisco. Winter had hardly begun to set in when they came through the mountains, but there was already snow and the nights were very cold. He could only imagine how truly bitter the cold was as a fellow passenger described the unfortunate wagon train whose members became lost in the Sierra Nevada, many of whom froze to death or died from starvation. Fortunately, progress had brought the railroads. His trip through the mountains was uneventful compared to those stories.

The water, the docks, and the salt air reopened the wound in Dodge's heart. Although he felt freer than he had in years, the sounds of the train had begun to stir the memories of his childhood and he knew he had to finally face them. He had to allow himself to sit and remember as best he could, rather than try to push those thoughts out of his head. He tried to envision his mother's face, his real mother. *If only I could remember my real name. I know she is probably dead, but surely I have brothers and sisters somewhere. I think I remember, if it isn't a dream, being in a house with other children. Were they put on the orphan trains, too? What happened that we had to be sent away?* Dodge had been haunted by the loss of his family, his mother. He had longed for those answers his whole life. He feared that the answers would never come.

Dodge didn't have any trouble remembering the orphanage or his adoptive mother, and unfortunately, his adoptive father.

He was reminded, once again, that he needed to write a letter to Sara. However, a letter to Cheri was definitely in order. He needed to let her know where he was in case she needed him. He also wanted to know about the progress of the store, if there were any problems, and news of events in Lawton.

Dodge hadn't arrived in San Francisco at the best time. Most of the debris from the last earthquake had been cleared, but much of the city had been destroyed. The buildings that had fallen were undergoing new construction and repair. San Francisco was slowly returning to normal, but much still needed to be done. There were detours everywhere, and there were plenty of construction jobs available.

After living in Texas, Dodge particularly enjoyed the cool, almost chilly, weather. He'd never had Chinese food and found that he loved it. There was always the smell of fresh baking bread and coffee in the crisp air. Texas had mostly been settled by English or German immigrants, with a spattering of other nationalities, while California seemed to be inhabited by many people from all over the world. He found the mixture of the cultures fascinating. Many of the Chinese people, who had helped to build the railroads, settled in California. Evidence of their culture was everywhere.

One particular disadvantage to the cool weather of northern California was that the water of the Pacific Ocean was very cold. His job on the boat was cold, cold work. He had developed a cough right away, and couldn't seem to shake it.

Dodge took a room in a large boarding house. His was one of the few rooms with a door and balcony, and it was on the west side of the house overlooking the bay. He sat on that balcony almost every evening. He had seen fog in Galveston, but had never seen anything like the mysterious black fog that rolled into San Francisco Bay. It was like a huge thick dark wall that just floated in over the water. He could also watch the giant freighters off in the distance coming and going to destinations all over the world. The setting sun over the Pacific Ocean cast the most vibrant gold, red, and pink colors he'd ever seen.

Dodge decided against the lighthearted ambition to pan for gold. After a visit to one of the land offices, he had an opportunity to observe some of the rugged old miners, still clinging to dreams of the Gold Rush days, living and working and staking their claims up in the mountains. It helped to change his mind, as he could see only trouble from such a dangerous endeavor.

He decided instead that he was going to see more of the state. Trolley cars and trains moved people all over the cities and the state, so he decided against buying another horse and began to take advantage of the trolley system. Living at the boarding house didn't allow for a convenient place to stable a horse, anyway. He was within walking distance to the docks, and he could take a trolley car anywhere else he might want to go. He would buy a horse only if the need arose.

One quiet evening while sitting on his balcony watching and feeling the warmth of the sunset, he felt peace spread through him. He felt himself let go, finally knowing that there must have been a powerful reason that he, and probably his siblings, had been put on that train. Perhaps his father had died, or maybe his parents were sick, or maybe like the Gurganis family, they hoped for their children to escape a dreadful illness or have a better life. Whatever the reason, he could finally accept it. Deep inside, he truly felt he had been loved, and was but an unfortunate victim of terrible circumstances.

Chapter Forty-eight

Although he couldn't communicate it, there were times when Mike's mind was clear. Those were the times when he was so frustrated, painfully aware of his condition and of his surroundings. He wished that he could be back on the ranch sitting on the porch, enjoying the day instead of being confined to a wheel chair and at the mercy of nurses and hotel staff.

For some reason, everyone thought he enjoyed being out on the balcony that was located just off his suite. He didn't. There wasn't anything pleasurable about watching the traffic and listening to all the roar of people, horses, motorcars and the like. He had always enjoyed the out of doors, the fresh air, trees, the smells of nature, but not this.

Most of the time the sun was too hot to be comfortable. He was left out there too long and too often, until sweat ran down his sides. Trying to protest did no good. No one paid any attention to his mumblings.

As much as anything he hated for them to talk to him like he was a baby or as if he weren't sitting right in the same room with them. *Damn it! I'm right here and I'm not a damn baby!* It was bad enough to endure being bathed and diapered.

The weather is a little cooler out here today. This might not be so bad. If they'll just let me have a decent meal, I'd be happy. Man, a good steak sure would taste good about now. It has been ages since I had a steak. Wonder what they'll bring. Probably more mush, for God's sake, that crappy mush. A man can't live on mush!

৪৩

The nurse went out on the balcony to check on Mike. She didn't expect a response, but when she touched his shoulder, she knew he had passed away. "God bless your soul, Mr. Terrell." Sometime in those last few hours that tough old Texan had taken his last breath. His ordeal was over.

The nurse set about finding the contact information and sending a rider out to notify Sara Cain and B.G. Steven.

Sara knew the minute the rider approached that he was bringing the notification they'd been expecting. A quick glance at the message confirmed her suspicions. She handed it back to the rider and gave him directions to the

Steven's house. He was kind enough to ride on out there to deliver it to B.G. and Johanna.

B.G.'s reaction to seeing the rider was the same as Sara's. He had known this news was coming. Sara had recently visited Mike and came out to let him know it would be soon. Now that it was official, B.G. had mixed emotions. He had never expected anything from Mike, but had never expected his family to suffer financially because of him, either.

He assumed there would be a letter arriving any day from Mike's attorney about the reading of Mike's will. B.G. didn't think there would be anything to it or anything left. Everything Mike had, in the end, was tied up in that ranch and it all went to the university. The piece of land that Mike had given to him wasn't his to keep, it never had been. He had lost the use of it long before he ever expected, though, which was the main issue, the most damaging and costly thing of all. Then, to make matters worse, Mike sent them all off on that needless trail drive and caused B.G. to take a loss on the sale of his cattle. No, B.G. wasn't feeling a sense of loss at Mike's death, rather indifference. Any sadness at all was sadness and disappointment for what he'd thought there had been, which apparently didn't exist at all. Regardless of his bitterness, B.G. never failed to appreciate the many things Mike had done for him. He owed his life to Mike and he knew that.

Johanna sympathized with her husband, who was normally a very softhearted, kind, loving person. The same reasons for B.G.'s bitterness made her angry, also. "It is too bad we can't have fond memories of someone who was so well thought of, who meant so much to us," she said to her husband.

When the notice came, B.G. couldn't make himself go. "I'm not going to go there and listen to what a wonderful person Mike was for donating the ranch to the university. I'm not going. If there is something I need to know Sara can deliver the message," he said out loud.

B.G. had just spent the last few days moving his cattle again. This time he moved them back to his own pastures. The other pastures were as dry as his own and he felt it important that they be on his land if he was going to start feeding or selling them. David wasn't going to be around much longer. He needed to move them while he still had some help.

There was still no rain. In addition to the cattle, his concerns now included the creek level dropping lower by the day.

Sara went to the reading. She didn't expect anything from Mike at all, but went in case there were some other requests from Mike. She had wondered where Mike would be buried and was surprised to learn that it was at a big cemetery in Austin rather than the little cemetery there near Sandy Creek. "One would think he would want to be buried where he had lived his whole life," Sara sighed aloud, "The era of Mike Terrell and the Terrell ranch is over."

There were no requests, nothing that Mike wanted done on his behalf, and B.G. had been correct, everything was left to the university. B.G. didn't attend the reading or the funeral.

The next morning B.G. hitched his wagon. He was going to the feed store in a nearby town. The need to feed the cattle overpowered his desire to resist. The cattle had to eat. They needed feed and hay. He had prepared himself to make use of the peach money, although not mentioning it to Johanna. He was forced to use it. There was no other way, and he didn't have the heart to tell her right then, and see the expression of concern in her eyes.

He would have to start selling a few cattle here and there in order to buy feed. Along with everything else, cattle prices were down, too. He hated to sell the cattle at those low prices. So many ranchers were selling off their stock at the same time that it was causing the prices to drop dramatically.

B.G. was worried about leaving his son and pregnant wife for an entire day. Under other circumstances he would let Joseph ride along with him and help his dad take care of business in town. It was too close to Johanna's time. She couldn't ride in the wagon for that distance, especially on those bumpy roads. Joseph was told to keep an eye on his mother.

"Joe, stay here at the house; don't go off anywhere. If anything happens, you run get Sara Cain, as fast as you can," B.G. instructed his son.

Chapter Forty-nine

Suddenly, Dodge was overwhelmed by the desire to see Sara Cain. He awakened from what seemed like a dream. His mind was filled with thoughts of Sara again, now fully awake. It seemed strange that all this time he'd been away from her he had never felt so compelled to go home.

The time he had spent in San Francisco had served more than to satisfy his curiosity about California. To his relief he'd been able to come to terms with his childhood, and the loss of his real family. He also recognized that while he had lost his family, he'd been one of the fortunate ones who ultimately found someone who really cared for and loved him, Henry Freeze. He could finally embrace that knowledge and let the rest go. Dodge had found true peace at long last.

Perhaps that feeling of peace had opened his eyes to how much he still loved Sara and how much he missed her. Perhaps this new inner peace would enable him to be near her again, without so much heartache. Even if it still meant they couldn't be together, he didn't want to stay away any longer. It was time to go home.

A letter would be in order. After all this time, he would sit down and write a letter to Sara. He would keep it brief, as it would be much easier to tell her everything face to face. He actually looked forward to telling her about the ladies, the trip through west Texas, the Indians, Oklahoma, the store, and now, about California.

He would also write a letter to Cheri. It was time he gave her his blessing on her marriage to Eli Ayers. A pang of jealously reminded him that he'd had his chance, but left for California instead. She couldn't have been expected to wait forever, especially since he'd never given her any encouragement about their arrangement. Besides, he truly loved another woman. It would hardly have been fair to her. The letter about the birth of the baby had sealed that for certain, anyway. Dodge couldn't imagine Cheri with a baby, but she and Eli had a baby and had named him Dodge, which made him proud. He would stop in Lawton on his way to Texas. He wanted to see the baby at least once, and see Cheri one last time. Eli was a good, hardworking man. He would make her happy. Dodge had no doubt that the store would continue to be successful in their hands and decided he would make arrangements to transfer full ownership to Cheri. His days in Lawton were over.

The doctor in San Francisco told Dodge that a drier, warmer climate would help his cough. It seemed there were many good reasons to head back now. The climate in the Hill Country was plenty dry. He remembered how pleasant the seasons were, not too cold, not too hot. It reminded him of standing barefoot in Sandy Creek on a hot day, wading in the cool clear water. He was also reminded of the cool crisp autumn mornings in Texas.

He suspected his cough had actually been caused by the dust in Oklahoma, but couldn't know for sure. He didn't have the cough before then. Either way, the climate would be better in Texas.

Dodge had loved working on the fishing boat. He loved San Francisco, the trolley cars, the Chinese food; he didn't even mind the occasional tremors he'd learned were similar to small earthquakes. They did little or no damage, but were unsettling, yet exciting. Afterward, everyone told tales of their tremor or quake experiences for days on end.

Dodge's boss and landlady received the news of his departure reluctantly. He and his landlady had established a bond between them. She was a dear motherly person, looking after his room and belongings when he was out at sea, sometimes for days at a time. She would always make a special meal for him when he returned. They often shared tea in the evenings. Her tea was quite unique, served up with a belt of whiskey and lemon and a little bit of tea. Those big juicy yellow lemons were one of the many nice things about California, plus the fragrance from all the fruit trees that filled the air throughout the region. The fresh fruit and vegetables and seafood were plentiful. He would definitely miss the food.

His boss hated to lose a good seaman and fisherman. Dodge likened him to the old ship captains in Galveston, tough as nails and fearless. His hands were big and rough, his skin red and rugged. His eyes revealed a kindhearted soul that enjoyed and loved life to the fullest. The captain had spent his entire life on a fishing boat. His family came to America as fishermen, and they all worked together in their seafood company.

Dodge dropped the two letters at the post office early in the morning on his last day of work. At the end of that week, he would board an eastbound train and leave San Francisco and California forever.

Chapter Fifty

As difficult as it was for Sara to make the final decision to sell the hotel and general store, the sign was now on the door. An advertisement had also been placed in the Austin newspaper. The decision met with Abel's approval, as he could see as well as Sara that the community was failing. Actually, theirs was the only business left.

They both realized it was unlikely the business would sell, but they set out to make needed repairs and spruce up the property.

David had given his notice and planned to leave soon. Making use of his help while he was still available was essential.

While David and Abel worked on the building, Sara boarded a train for Galveston. Before exploring opportunities in Austin, she wanted to do so in Galveston.

She anticipated finding remnants of the destruction left by the hurricane, but to her relief, there was little that hadn't been cleared away. Most of the construction and restoration had been done.

Sara was compelled to visit the old strand and pier area near where her parents' store used to be. It was the first time she had returned to the island since the hurricane and the death of her father. Familiar places brought back memories of special times in her life. Surprisingly, the damage hadn't been as extensive there as on the rest of the island. Almost all the buildings with minor destruction had been restored. Her parents store was completely gone, however. She would never know the extent of the damage, but whatever it was, it was too much to restore. The building had been demolished and hauled away. An empty lot sat in its place. Sara didn't have the heart to sell it yet.

The island had changed since the hurricane. A sea wall had been constructed to help protect the island from future hurricanes. Sea Wall Boulevard and a wide sidewalk extended for miles along the coast. There were many businesses, shops, hotels and restaurants along the wall. The contrast of the island city to the surroundings back home was dramatic. There were so many conveniences that didn't exist in their remote area.

Sara found a building along the sea wall facing out across the gulf. It had a large storage area upstairs that could be converted to an apartment. She could smell the salt air and hear the gulls. She hadn't decided the specific type of business they would establish, but she definitely decided on the building. Sara wasted no time opening an account with a newly founded bank in Galveston, arranged for a transfer of the funds to purchase the building and signed the papers. In a few days the building would be hers.

ಶ೦ೞ

Katherine's vault and others in the cemetery had remained undisturbed throughout the hurricane and aftermath. Although he would never be found or be buried there, Sara made arrangements to have her father's memorial placed beside her mother's and completed with the date, September 8, 1900.

Sara found herself on a train again at night. The last time she slept on a train was a very sad time. On that trip she was so tired from the trip itself, the hard work at the store and hotel, and the emotional drain of losing her mother that she was overtaken by sleep. This time she was so excited that she couldn't sleep at all. Imagining the opportunities from tourism that would come along the sea wall, her thoughts became focused entirely on Galveston. All thoughts of moving to Austin had vanished. She spent the entire trip planning and envisioning their future.

When the train finally arrived at the depot, Sara was surprised to find Luke Matthews waiting for her. Many things instantly ran through her mind about why

Luke was there instead of Abel, but when there was no smile on Luke's face, she knew something was terribly wrong.

Luke held back his own tears as he haltingly explained that Abel had fallen from the roof of the hotel and had sustained terrible injuries. The doctor had come out, but didn't give them much encouragement.

"Are you telling me that Abel is dying?" Sara screamed, as panic gripped her. "Where is he?"

Luke had come to pick her up in her motorcar and drove back to the hotel as fast as it would travel. Never mind the bumpy roads. He explained to her that Abel had not regained consciousness, and tried to describe the details of his fall and injuries.

Sara hurried into the kitchen. Abel had been carried into the little room at the back of the hotel where they used to sleep before the upstairs was added. It was also the room where Dodge stayed, and later, Etta and Daniel, before they moved into their home.

Abel looked as though he was merely asleep. It was hard to believe that he could be hurt so badly, but he was, and he never regained consciousness. Sara was by his side every moment, watching every breath until there was a gasp and Abel's chest didn't rise again.

A small group of the residents who still remained gathered at the little cemetery. With kind words and prayers spoken by Luke Matthews, Abel was laid to his final rest among cherished friends and loved ones, in the little cemetery there by Sandy Creek.

Chapter Fifty-one

Relieved to return to find his family safe and sound, B.G. exchanged grateful, loving hugs with Joseph and Johanna.

Joseph ran outside to help unload the wagon. He liked to climb up on the wagon and ride alongside his dad whenever he could. They rode over to the barn where B.G. stacked the bags and pushed most of the hay off the back of the wagon. "Let's leave the rest of the hay on the wagon, Joe. We'll take it out to the cattle in the morning."

That next morning David arrived with the news about Abel Cain. B.G. immediately took Johanna over to stay with Sara until after the funeral. Because of her own condition, she couldn't be much help to Sara, but she was there for support. Etta pitched in to help with everything else.

There were all the usual things that have to be done when someone dies. Sara had to make a trip to the lawyer's office in Austin. She was not one to put off taking care of important business. Everything needed to be changed, the will needed to be probated, her own will needed to be rewritten, and arrangements made for a headstone. Sara couldn't make herself believe or accept that she was attending to these things, that Abel was actually gone.

Johanna tried to help by going to the hotel and general store every day while Sara took care of items that had to be addressed and made the necessary trips to Austin. She was surprised to see how little stock there was left on the shelves in the store. For some reason it was something that had gone unnoticed. She would have done anything for Sara after all that Sara had done for her and B.G., but she could tell it was time for the baby at any moment. A surprise birth at the hotel wasn't a good idea.

Joseph needed his mother at home when he came home from school. Even though he was old enough to be there alone, Johanna was determined that he would do his studies every day. He was a good student and she had plans for him. He was going to be more than a rancher or farmer. He was going to have an education and not have a life that depended on the weather. There were a number of reasons Johanna needed to be at home.

David's arrival with the news about Abel had interrupted B.G. before he had an opportunity to tell Johanna the bad news about the cost of the feed and hay. It had taken almost all of the peach and pecan money to pay for it. There were only a few dollars left. He knew she would be upset. That money was needed for the household and the little that was left was saved for Joseph's education. Unfortunately, there was less and less left.

If it didn't rain soon B.G. didn't know what they would do. Johanna's fall garden wouldn't do as well, either. Hauling water from the creek took a whole day by the time they filled the tubs a bucket at a time. They were reluctant to use their well water, but it would be a bucket at a time, too. At least the weather was cooler so the garden wouldn't burn up so quickly.

The almanac stated there would be rain in the fall, so B.G. checked the sky each morning hoping for any sign of a cloud. A few mild fronts had come through, but none had brought rain.

B.G. and Joseph drove the wagon in to pick up Johanna from the general store. Sara had put a closed sign on the door at the hotel. Although there were no hotel guests anymore, the sign would allow Sara to liquidate the furnishings without having to accommodate guests at the same time.

Johanna announced that the pains had begun and expected it would go on all night. She had hopes that it would be a little girl and had already picked a name. She made supper for B.G. and Joseph and went to her room to wait, while B.G. went for the midwife.

This was Johanna's fourth birth. She hoped it would be easier than the others. A twinge of fear flashed through her mind. She hadn't felt the baby move in a few days, but assumed it had been getting ready for the birth.

Her fears were realized when after a night of labor, the baby finally came, but never drew a breath. It was the little girl that Johanna had hoped for. She was given the name Mary Jane.

B.G. made a coffin and a marker, and Mary Jane Steven was buried next to her sister, Sara Elizabeth. Once again, within a few weeks, Luke Matthews helped to ease the pain of another lost loved one.

Three dead babies were enough to drain the last bit of spirit from Johanna. In a moment of total despair, she quietly told B.G., "There will be no more babies."

From that day forward, neither of them touched each other, maybe a brief hug, but although B.G. understood, he also wanted to avoid the desire that came from touching his wife. Johanna wanted her husband to hold her, to kiss her, but she knew it was easier for her than for him. She would hold herself away. If it could be expected of him she could abide, as well.

Chapter Fifty-two

The eastbound train from San Francisco gallantly performed its struggle up one side of each mountain and sped rapidly down the other. Up and over snowcapped mountains, through the tall pines and firs, cottonwoods, and bright yellow aspens, the rails were endless, crossing deep caverns and streams over sky-high bridges. Dodge was no exception among his fellow passengers. He couldn't pull his eyes away from the window. It had been nighttime when he went through there before. He was grateful for daylight. The natural beauties of nature were on display in the bright sunshine.

He played over in his mind what it would be like to see Cheri again and her child. He especially looked forward to seeing the boy, his namesake. "One day at a time," he told himself, as his mind raced on to thoughts of Texas and Sandy Creek. "One day at a time."

Dodge stepped outside the back door of his passenger car to watch as the eastbound train stopped to meet the westbound train. Unknown to Dodge, or anyone else, a robber climbed up on the tinderbox while the train was stopped. When the train approached the next milepost, where the rest of the gang was waiting, the robber drew down on the engineer and wounded him in the leg. The engineer returned fire and shot the robber dead, but not before the rest of the gang boarded the train to rob the passengers. The Wells Fargo Express messenger, who had the payroll, refused to open the door. Hearing gunfire, Dodge quickly ran inside, locking the door behind him, and just as quickly, ran to the other end of the car and locked that door.

The exchange of gunfire continued until a posse arrived, at which time the crew shot and injured another member of the gang. The rest of the robbers fled, with the posse and deputies in pursuit.

The body of the dead robber was left by the tracks to await the undertaker. The injured one was taken into custody.

The passengers in Dodge's car immediately began to praise him for saving their valuables and their lives. Humbly, he accepted their praise, but assured them he did little more than lock the doors, which could have been penetrated easily, had the robbers wanted to do so. Fortunately, they had been more interested in the express money.

Dodge spent the rest of the trip thinking about the incident and wondering about the many events in his life and how all those events didn't seem to happen to average people. *Why me? It seems I was destined from the beginning to have such a crazy life.*

Dodge hardly recognized Lawton except for the red dust cloud that still hung over the city. In such a short time, Lawton had spread across the horizon.

Cheri was standing behind the counter closing out for the day. She looked up as he entered. That same beautiful smile spread across her face as she greeted him. That same familiar feeling warmed him deep inside – just as it had the last time he saw her. The ending would be different this time. She was a married woman and mother.

Eli came through the storage room door just at that moment with a young boy by his side. Dodge knew instantly that he was young Dodge, but he also knew instantly that little Dodge was not Eli's, but his own son. The boy looked exactly like him and nothing at all like Cheri or Eli. He suspected that Eli must know, and was grateful that the man who married Cheri had made the choice to accept her son. It clearly appeared he loved the boy and the boy loved him.

With both Dodge and the boy in the same room together, Dodge could see the stricken expression on Cheri's face. Of course Cheri knew, but had failed to realize just how strong the resemblance would be. Her eyes darted toward Eli, who seemed not to notice at all. He extended his hand and with his other hand, reached for

Dodge's shoulder and began patting him and shaking his hand at the same time.

A sigh of relief escaped Dodge's throat. The muscles in Cheri's face began to relax.

Young Dodge Ayers was introduced to his Uncle Dodge Blackburn and they became instant friends. Dodge called young Dodge his "Little Buddy" and they spent the next three days side by side. During that time, Dodge transferred ownership of the store to Cheri. He took the time to visit a lawyer to make a will, which he had never done. He left any and all of his estate to young Dodge. At the time, Dodge didn't know the extent of his own worth, that he was an heir to the fortune of Henry Freeze. It would have made no difference. He loved that little boy and everything he represented.

It was evident that Little Bit hadn't forgotten Dodge. He raised his head over and over and shook it from side to side in recognition. Dodge wouldn't attempt to ride him back to Texas, but made arrangements for him to ride on the train as far as the stop nearest to the Cain Hotel and home. Home being wherever Sara Cain was.

His heart had begun to beat a little faster as every minute passed.

Chapter Fifty-three

Even though Lawton was very close to Fort Sill and good law enforcement had been established, like any other big developing city, a criminal element had begun to thrive there. No Man's Land to the west and the territory beyond were central to many states. Gangs and criminals could hide out there, make runs into various towns, rob a bank, a train, an express office, and the like, then high tail it back.

The tales of No Man's Land had become the stuff of legends, and many exciting articles appeared in the newspapers. There was an abundance of columnists and photographers in Lawton on any given day.

The same legends, and facts, of course, brought Federal Agents to Lawton in search of those criminals. The agents made trips into No Man's Land and the New Mexico Territory, as well as staking out the local saloons, brothels and the typical places criminals might frequent.

In pursuit of the gang that had been robbing trains, once again Federal Agents Reed and Jackson were assigned the mission that others had failed to accomplish.

Coming face to face with Dodge Blackburn in Lawton, Oklahoma was the last thing they expected.

"What are you fellas doing here?" Dodge exclaimed, still thinking they were cowhands.

After all these years and surprise encounters, the two of them decided it was time to come clean with Dodge. They confessed that they were Federal Agents and that their meetings over the years weren't totally coincidence. Yes, coincidence that Dodge was involved, but not them. They were on assigned missions each time.

The agents began to describe their encounters. "When we met at Sandy creek, we were in pursuit of a gang of bank robbers. As it turned out, it was the very gang and crime of which we were all accused. It was our reason for being at the encampment. After leaving you and Cheri at San Solomon Springs, we went to Texas Ranger Dred Hill's office to clear your name and help the Ranger capture the real outlaws who had robbed several other banks. Our efforts uncovered the robbers' hideout and facilitated their arrest."

When they met in west Texas, they had been in pursuit of Maw'wat and his band of renegades. "Dodge, you saved us the trouble of a confrontation and hauling him in. You pursued and killed one of the most ruthless, dangerous criminals ever."

"So you were the ones out in the desert. I thought there was someone out there. I kept smelling food and hoping like hell it was someone coming to help. Why didn't you tell me about it then? Well, I guess you couldn't. I was sure glad to see you when you finally did show your faces."

"At the time, we weren't sure who you were. We couldn't see you, and until we heard all the gunshots, we were waiting to see who you were. We didn't want to get bush- whacked."

"We are in Lawton because we have been follow-ing the gang that just recently robbed an eastbound train en route to here, but have been robbing trains in Colorado and New Mexico for some time now, then disappearing into No Man's Land."

"I was on that train!" Dodge described the event in detail. He also described the gunmen, as he had gotten a very good look at some of them. He told them about lock-ing the doors in the passenger car and how relieved they all were when the posse showed up. "I'm too old to be chasing rascals like that anymore," Dodge said.

"What brings you back to Lawton?" Jackson asked.

Dodge shared his reason for being in Lawton, and told them the outcome of Cheri's story, about the store, and about Eli and Little Dodge. He went on to tell them about California and about his plan to return to the Cain Hotel and to Sandy Creek.

Dodge was amused that they had been so convincing about their identities as cowhands. After all this time, he finally knew, or sort of knew, who they really were. One thing for sure, he was very glad to learn that they weren't bank robbers.

Their goodbyes were said, with each doubting it would be the last time their paths would cross.

"See you later, Reed and Jackson. No last name, huh?"

Chapter Fifty-four

It was settled for certain. After so many years, Sara would be leaving the little unnamed community nestled by Sandy Creek. A place where she thought she would live for the rest of her life.

She had already purchased the building in Galveston, but never got to share that news with Abel.

Sara had decided that whether she opened a business or not, she was going to Galveston. Staying where she was, in that dying place, was out of the question. She could imagine herself an aging old widow alone in that big building, which no doubt would begin to deteriorate. By all indications it was only a matter of time before everyone else would be gone from there. There were towns fairly close that could be relied upon for supplies and food. She refused to feel guilty.

There was only one offer for the purchase of the building. A demolition company wanted the lumber. Sara had to think about that for a while. It was one thing to leave, but quite another to actually demolish the building that had been lovingly built with their own hands, and with their hopes and dreams of the future. Further thought about it changed her mind. Perhaps to have the building dismantled and totally cleared away would be better than having it stand empty and slowly deteriorating.

Thinking about the lumber being reused filled Sara with new inspiration. She wouldn't sell the lot where her family's store had sat in Galveston. She would rebuild on it, rebuild her father's store, just exactly as it used to be. It would be a memorial to her parents.

There was only one issue left that must be addressed. Etta had no family and must be persuaded to go with her to Galveston. With the exception of Dodge Blackburn, Sara had no family left, either. It had begun to appear that she would never see him again. She refused to leave Etta there alone. They would go together to Galveston to start a new life.

Word traveled fast. Sara was surprised at how many people showed up to purchase the furnishings. The demolition company had removed the counters and cabinets from the hotel and general store. Sara's bedroom furniture was all that remained, and it had been promised to Johanna. The other furnishings were gone in one day. The shell of the building stood alone.

Looking at the empty shell, she remembered the wonder and excitement they felt when it was all being built, living in the tent and the wagon, how her father was there with them supervising the construction. They stood over a makeshift table made from a sawhorse and piece of lumber, with catalogs and papers spread before them, where they ordered the supplies and furnishings for the general store. She remembered hauling water up from Sandy Creek before the well and cistern were dug and bricked.

It was when they first met Luke Matthews. He was coming there to locate the farm he'd inherited from a relative, such a young man. Like everyone who initially came there, Luke had high hopes. His dream was for a church and schoolhouse. He was able to realize his dream, just as they had realized theirs. But like the demise of their dreams, the demise of the school came about, as too few children remained there to hold classes, so the remaining students had begun traveling farther to another larger school nearby. Luke still held Sunday services, but came there only once a month on the route of the churches he served.

Etta didn't take much persuading. She was relieved that Sara finally invited her to go. "I thought you was neva gonna ask," Etta replied, in her charming way, a little bit scolding, a little bit laughing. So it was done. Etta would join her in the new adventure. Coaxing her to ride in the motorcar would be another matter. Etta was superstitious about the motorcar. It would be a long trip to Galveston.

The motorcar was overloaded with boxes and trunks. All final arrangements had been made. B.G. and Joseph were going to pick up any mail that might be left in the box. With one last visit to the cemetery and tearful goodbyes, Sara and Etta were off.

Joseph stood and watched until the motorcar disappeared in the dust.

Chapter Fifty-five

All the way from California and all the way to Sandy Creek from Lawton, Dodge hoped he'd seen the last of trains for a while. He stepped off at a whistle stop just an hour away from his destination. The closer he got to the Cain Hotel the more anxious he'd become, hardly able to wait while an attendant brought Little Bit around to the platform.

It would require patience to ride along at Little Bit's slow pace, but it had taken this long and he could be patient a little longer, while his old friend proudly carried him home.

Dodge took in the fresh Texas air that came as autumn approached. The familiarity of the landscape made him homesick while he was right in the midst of it all, the cedar brush, mesquite and oak trees. The fragrance and the cool crisp air filled his senses.

Little Bit made his way along the rough, rugged, old wagon path from the train stop. The soil had eroded away, leaving slabs of granite and sandstone exposed, much as it was everywhere else in that terrain. The path, now seldom traveled, was overgrown and barely visible.

Dodge decided to postpone his arrival for just a bit longer and take the cut-off over to the encampment. He wondered if anyone he knew might still be there, though that would be unlikely after all these years. He imagined it would be much bigger and that there would be many more families.

They had ridden far enough that they should have reached the encampment when Dodge realized he was in the very spot where it used to be. There was scant evidence that it had ever been there, but some of the most worn areas were still distinguishable. The path to the creek was definitely evident and the rock remains of the little dock were still there. *I wonder when they all finally left, where they all went?* A picture of Rosie and Cheri's colorful wagon flashed through his mind, as well as the terrifying night the posse rode in and arrested him.

The crossing bridge at the road was also still there and Dodge and Little Bit set out across it, detouring on the other side of the creek along the bank toward the Terrell ranch.

Dodge soon learned that the Terrell ranch no longer existed, either, the same as the encampment no longer existed. The huge gate, which had been emblazoned with the Terrell ranch brand, and which had once loomed impressively at the entrance, was no longer there at all. Instead, there was a cattle guard and a padlocked iron gate with a small no trespassing sign attached. In the distance, he barely got a glimpse of the ranch house, which appeared to be vacant. The grounds around the entire area were empty.

Uneasiness settled in the pit of his stomach. *There is no reason that I should expect things to remain the same after being gone for so long.* He began to wonder what else might have changed. Who was alive and who was dead.

The road from the Terrell ranch had always been the most traveled route. On the other side of Sandy Creek, just beside the road, was the little cemetery. Around the bend past the cemetery, the trees and brush cleared, and in that clearing many years before, was where the community had been established. The road went on through there and beyond. It went on in the direction of Fort Mason, where it forked north. He remembered that road very well and the day he set out to find the ladies and the Cain's money.

Do I dare? Dodge stood at the gate of the little cemetery. He could see from the gate that there were many more headstones and markers than he remembered. He slowly, tentatively stepped through the gate, a sense of dread rising in his throat. He saw Guenther Gurganis' place of rest, then Daniel, Etta's husband. He was surprised and saddened to see the names of two Steven children,

"Babies." Then his knees almost buckled when he saw the headstone of Abel Cain. *Oh, my God! Oh, Sara!*

Dodge sprinted through the gate and down the road, leaving Little Bit behind. Rounding the bend, he stopped in his tracks. There was almost nothing there, no one, no life. The old blacksmith shop was boarded and locked. The rock church was still there, and the fallen cistern, but nothing else. Where the hotel and general store once stood was nothing more than evidence of a foundation and a few piles of lumber, the mailbox and an old wagon.

Dodge looked beyond at the few abandoned houses, as that slight sense of dread in the pit of his stomach now totally consumed him.

If not for a tall boy walking down the road toward him, Dodge would have ridden off in the opposite direction, without any destination in mind, desperate to know where to go, what to do, what had happened, where Sara had gone. He stood watching as the boy approached, said nothing, and walked toward the mailbox, which was the only thing still there.

"Excuse me, young man, do you know where Mrs. Cain is?" The boy didn't answer and hurried back down the road with the mail he'd taken from the box. Dodge followed far enough back as not to frighten him. When a house appeared in the distance the lad began to run to the house and into the door.

Not knowing what to expect, Dodge was relieved when B.G. Steven came out the door with a shotgun in his hands.

"I'm Dodge Blackburn, B.G. Do you remember me?"

Chapter Fifty-six

The county agent confirmed B.G.'s suspicions. The steer had anthrax. It had been suspected for some time that severe drought conditions somehow stirred up the spores that caused it. Since the ground was pure dust, it was no surprise. The heat from summer hadn't let up, save for a few mornings that were a bit cooler. He'd been watching the skies and praying every day that rain would come. It was bad enough that he hadn't noticed the symptoms earlier, to maybe save some of the cattle. Now he regretted that he hadn't sold off his herd like most all the other ranchers had done. Bad prices would have been better than no price.

The question is; how do I tell Johanna? This is the final blow. We can't recover from this. We are not going to have the money to make our loan payment. I have to go find work or we won't even have money for food.

B.G. knew they would to have to leave the ranch. He also knew they would have to move to a city where there would be work. The only thing he had ever known was cattle and ranching, unable to imagine what kind of work he could find. He wasn't proud. He would do whatever he needed to do.

Joseph could help, too. He was old enough and there were jobs in the city that didn't exist in the country. B.G. knew that boys in the city sold newspapers, shined shoes, delivered groceries and any number of odd jobs. As much as it would pain Johanna, college would just have to wait.

His biggest hope was that one of the neighboring ranchers might take over his loan and pay him a little equity so he wouldn't totally lose everything. It would give them enough money to move, at least.

Johanna sat quietly, tears streaming down her face, as he told her the bad news. He quickly shared his ideas about moving and selling the place, finding work, hoping it would lift her spirits, but it didn't seem to help. B.G. wanted terribly to hold her, to comfort her. He couldn't stop himself, stepping toward her, reaching for her.

Johanna couldn't resist. After so very long and their strong need for each other, even she fell vulnerable to her emotions and the strength of her husband's arms. They lay together for hours, holding each other, fulfilling what their abstinence had withheld.

They both knew they would move to a city somewhere. They would go where their son, Joseph, could go to school. Together, they would make certain his life wouldn't be altered by this unhappy event.

B.G. visited his neighbors letting them know about the anthrax. It was the responsible thing to do. He also told them that he needed to sell his small ranch, and was hopeful someone could take over the loan. Fortunately, he found that person, so part of the problem was solved. His neighbor, concerned over anthrax in his own pastures and feeling responsible for renting his pastures to B. G., agreed to assume the loan. He had sufficient land that he would be able to quarantine those pastures for a few years. It was an unexpected gesture, a blessing that would leave them with enough money to move and get established somewhere else.

It was decided they would move to Austin. Surely a town the size of Austin would offer some type of employment for B.G., and Joseph could finish school and attend college there. Johanna would take in sewing, as she had become quite the seamstress under the tutelage of Sara Cain. She knew how to design and make patterns as well as anyone.

B.G. made a promise to himself. If it was the last thing he ever did, Joseph would finish school and Johanna would have a better life in the future.

The most painful problem still remained. The cattle had to be destroyed.

On that somber day the sky was crystal clear. B.G. stood silently, leaning back on his heels with a rifle in his hands. The hot Texas sun beat down on the brim of his hat. He was looking across at her as she stood on the other side, her eyes fixed on the deep trench between them. He could see her thin frame as the wind pressed her dress against her body. His heart ached for the sadness that was etched in her face by the loss of the babies, her father, her home, now the cattle and their livelihood. Surely this was never the life Johanna would have chosen for herself or her family. These had been hard years for her, for everyone.

They could both hear the drovers off in the distance herding the last of the cattle toward them.

Chapter Fifty-seven

Prepared to check in for a long stay, Sara was impressed with the recently opened hotel. The interior and the furnishings even exceeded the exterior and were extravagant to the last detail. Opened eleven years after the hurricane, boldly facing the gulf, it was a symbol of the restoration of Galveston, both the city and the human spirit.

When the desk clerk assumed that Etta was her personal maid, Sara remained silent for fear Etta wouldn't be allowed to stay in the hotel. Many things had changed over the years, but some things hadn't changed enough. Neither of them wanted to draw attention to themselves. It made it easier to share a suite. Sara wanted to spare Etta any unpleasantness, knowing the struggles she already tried so hard to control.

The war and the thirteenth amendment that was intended to free the slaves provided only temporary prosperity, but soon resulted in the opposite outcome, especially in the South.

The clerk, other staff, and management could think whatever they wished.

It was a rare thing for a woman to be traveling alone, whether she brought her maid or not. It was even rarer for a woman to drive an automobile, though automobiles were much more common in Galveston than most places in Texas.

Sara's identity soon became known. Many remembered her father, of course, one of the wealthier, most respected men in the island city toward the end of the century, lost like so many, in the great hurricane.

Sara wasted no time tackling her plans. There were no problems at all in obtaining funding to do so.

Two large projects at the same time might make a person pause, but not Sara. She undertook both with ease, the reconstruction of her family's store, and the remodel of the building on the seawall. She'd decided there would be living quarters in both, but since the building on the seawall would be completed first and would be the place where she and Etta would open their business, it was decided to make it their home. Each of them would have a bedroom, with a joint balcony facing the gulf.

A decision hadn't been made about what she might do with the new building on Tremont Street, but construction wouldn't be complete for a while, and there was plenty of time to decide.

It was all so familiar to her, picking colors of paint, ordering cabinets, counters and supplies. It was fun choosing the merchandise, because she'd never ordered trinkets or beach clothing or the like. She even let Etta pick some island voodoo carvings, beads and "junk," as Sara called it.

Sara took a moment to reflect on everything that had been accomplished in those recent months since Abel's death. She felt like she was still living their dream, as if they had decided together to make a change, to start over. There hadn't been one moment that she hadn't been so busy, stayed so busy, that there was time to dwell on his death. She was surprised to be doing so well. Recognizing Etta's contribution was important. Her constant, nurturing presence had been a blessing.

Both Sara and Etta behaved like children at the furniture store. Buying all new bedroom furniture and linens, they each felt like a princess. Furnishing their entire apartment in a beach theme, colorful and sunny, made them both giddy.

Wealth wasn't a position that had influenced Sara's family. Humble, grateful and hardworking, were words that epitomized her father's character. He wasn't impressed by wealth other than the good that might come from it. His deeds were many, contributing huge sums to those in need. He judged himself by those deeds, his honor and his integrity.

Those attributes lived on in his daughter. Working in the little seaside shop with Etta would be fun and would keep them both busy. Income or profit from the shop, if any, would be a pleasant surprise, but Sara would resume her father's charitable work.

Living among the families in the community, seeing their struggles the last few years, knowing and loving the Steven family, especially Joseph, made Sara aware of another important use for her wealth. A scholarship fund would help more than anything. As for Joseph, a fund had already been established for his education, which was unknown to his parents or to him. She knew of his parents' struggles. The gift would be announced at the right time. Joseph was the closest Sara would ever come to having a child and she did not want to see him deprived.

Being the independent woman that she had been raised to be, self-reliant and adventurous, Sara took the women's suffrage movement seriously. Seeing it as an opportunity to contribute politically and to make a difference assured her involvement. She was in attendance at every meeting, at every rally, volunteering to take on issues and take on those who resisted women having the right to vote. Sara saw it as being no different than some attitudes towards the black people. Finding herself alone after Abel's death brought about a new independent spirit and determination, especially when it became evident that she had so few rights as a woman. She was more fortunate than most. *What must life be like for a woman with no husband and no money?* She resolved it would change in her lifetime.

Relaxing on her balcony, enjoying her coffee that morning, listening and watching the surf, Sara sat straight up in her chair. It suddenly came to her, like a lightning bolt. Her involvement with the women's suffrage movement had awakened her to the hardships women often suffered, no education, abusive husbands, widowhood with children and no income. There was so much more than the right to vote, which needed to be done in order to help women. Sara knew, finally, what her fortune and her name could help accomplish. As her mind continued to race with her new purpose, an entire mission materialized. The old building on Tremont Street, her father's store, could become a women's center, where they could receive assistance with education, health, abuse and the many issues that were unique to women. The construction was almost complete. A visit to the architect was the first order at hand. Some changes to the building needed to be made right away while the architect and construction crew were still there. The next step would be to call on her many friends and associates to rally their support and involvement. Furniture and volunteers would be the next items on her agenda. The Freeze Memorial Center for Women sounded wonderful. *Mother, you would be so proud of me. I wish we could share this dream.*

Sara wrote a letter to Johanna and her family, who had been collecting the mail from the hotel mailbox in her absence. It was time to furnish an address, let them know she and Etta were well, and send her love.

Dearest Johanna and B.G.,

So ardently I miss you and my darling Joseph. Our arrival in the coastal city met with that of the departing vacationers and beach goers.

We have made great progress on our home and shop. Sharing our home has been such a pleasure to us both. Etta brings light and joy to this and my world.

Mail will be received at the address enclosed herein. We will be anticipating same, upon your receipt of this post.

Very truly yours,
Sara Cain

Chapter Fifty-eight

It didn't take long for B.G. to find a home in Austin. He found one with a good amount of property that would allow them to feel like they were still in the country. It had a sweeping, rocky lot with room for a garden and many trees. Johanna could plant some fruit trees and have a few chickens. There were enough bedrooms that she could use one for a sewing room. The big back porch went all the way across the house. He knew she would love it.

While he was there he applied for several jobs, one of which seemed particularly promising. His history in the Texas Hill Country was favorable to the River Authority, as he was familiar with the countryside and both the Colorado River and the Llano River, and the many creeks that meandered through the hills and valleys. He was happy and eager to report the good news to Johanna, who had remained at home packing their belongings.

Even with the terrible setback of losing the cattle and being forced to give up their small ranch, B.G. remained optimistic about their future, although he would never forget the drastic measures that had brought them to this position. It made him sick to his stomach to even think about it. That was a heartbreaking day.

With the demise of the community, with the drought, and with the school closing, B.G. felt it time to accept that the family would be better off in the city. He knew Johanna would feel happier and safer, and would be relieved about Joseph's education. All of the things that had worked against their success might have some meaning for their life, something waiting in their future.

They managed to sell their equipment and some of their furnishings. The neighbors bought the chickens and other stock. Of course, all the cattle were already gone.

Their belongings would fit in to two wagons, one borrowed from a neighbor, who had pitched in to help. Joseph would drive one of the wagons and his dad would drive the other one.

Johanna continued her packing while B.G. shared his news. She pulled two wooden boxes from the floor of a closet, suddenly remembering the contents within were her mother's china. It had remained undisturbed ever since they left the Terrill ranch, hadn't even been unpacked or used. *It is coming out of the boxes when we get settled,* she promised herself.

B.G. and Joseph spent most of the day harvesting the garden. Then they visited the neighbors, sharing the vegetables among them and bidding their final farewells.

Joseph had checked out of school and was dreading going to a new school in the city. He saw himself as a country kid and was afraid he would be different from the city kids, that they wouldn't like him. His dad assured him it would all be okay, although "dad" was uneasy himself. B.G. had never lived in the city either, nor had a regular job that meant going to work at eight o'clock and working until five o'clock and answering to a boss who was there on the job with you. His job had been working from daylight until dark, and it was something different every day, from rounding up cattle to building fences. None of them had lived in the city. Even Johanna's family had lived on a farm in Tennessee.

They cleaned the house thoroughly, and raked and picked up the yard. Johanna wanted to leave the house clean. The neighbor who bought the place was going to rent it out.

The wagons were stacked high with boxes and furnishings. To avoid being crushed under the weight of the other belongings, the wooden boxes containing the china dishes were the last items to be secured.

Johanna stepped outside to steal a few minutes to walk down to the orchard. She stopped to look at the tree where she and B.G. had carved the date and their initials when they moved onto the ranch. Taking time to breathe it all in, she strolled to the back of the orchard to Pebble's grave and marker. She needed to say one last goodbye to Pebble before she left him forever. She had already been to the cemetery to say goodbye to her sweet babies and to her father. It was hard to leave them, not knowing when or if she would ever be there again.

Pulling away from their home reminded Johanna of the day that she and her father left their home in Tennessee. The house was all locked up and dark, the chickens Joseph couldn't catch still scratching around the yard, scattering when the wagons began to move.

When the day had finally come, B.G.'s optimism somehow spread to all of them. Johanna even felt a twinge of excitement thinking about the few days that she and her father spent in Austin so very long ago. She thought of her own words, "I could stay here forever," and remembered how much she'd loved Austin. She didn't know what might lie ahead for them, but she knew what she was gladly leaving behind.

"Johanna, look." B.G. pointed to the sky. Dark clouds had gathered quickly and were almost above them. A hard rain was approaching. They began to feel droplets as they hurried on down the road. B.G. stood up in the wagon and took his hat off, waving it at the sky. "Come on, pour down, you son of a gun! Now you come!"

ဆာၓ

Although the water level was still low in the creek, it was already flowing swiftly due to the heavy rains upstream. The route they had chosen took them over the old bridge near where the encampment used to be. Those old, seldom traveled country roads and bridges received very little maintenance. Ruts had developed around the ramps onto the bridge. The wagon took a hard jolt on the ruts, causing one of the boxes of china to bounce off the back of the wagon. It tumbled, unnoticed, down the embankment to the edge of the fast rising water. It came to rest beneath the narrow bridge that crossed over Sandy Creek.

Chapter Fifty-nine

It would be their last assignment. Both of them had decided, long ago, that they would retire at the same time. There was a special reason they made that decision, but it also just wouldn't be the same this late in the game, to have to get used to a new partner. Law enforcement had been good to both of them, especially in recent years. They had received more commendations than any other team, even meeting the President one time. They had visited every territory and almost every state in the union in pursuit of justice in the performance of their duty.

Reed and Jackson, together, had the extraordinary opportunity to witness close up the westward expansion of the country. They had met many people, some more than once, like their friend, Dodge Blackburn, who seemed to appear in the most unlikely places. They had captured or pursued some of the most dangerous, ruthless characters in the country, like the notorious Indian renegade,

Maw'wat, along with many train robbers and bank robbers.

They even took leave of their regular duties at one time to work on a clandestine operation for the President himself, concerning the war with Spain. It was one of their proudest accomplishments. The contribution was significant to the outcome of that war.

This most recent and last assignment was to capture a gang who especially liked robbing trains, as trains could be boarded and robbed as they moved through the countryside. Away from local law enforcement and visibility, they could board the trains and take any valuable cargo, sometimes including the personal possessions of the passengers, then escape into the countryside or into the mountains. So far this latest gang of robbers had managed to escape capture from all of the local law enforcement and the various posses who had pursued them.

That gang's reputation was well known to everyone in the West, and the reporters and newspapers from coast to coast had made their escapades legend.

On many occasions, the dead bodies of criminals were placed in caskets and left open for all to see. The photographs of the corpses were published in the newspapers; the more notorious they were, the better. If a criminal's true reputation didn't appear to be bad enough, the reporters would often embellish it.

The last train robbery had resulted in the death of one member of the gang and the injury and capture of another. By all reports several others were still at large. However, there was no way to know how many criminals actually hung out at Dead Man's Dugout. It was a fitting name that had been bestowed by the newspaper reporters to create drama and intrigue for their readers.

Fleeing into the vast territories or into No Man's Land had allowed them to disappear many times, thus the call for Reed and Jackson to step in. The capture of the gang would be the final feather in their hat.

Hoping to prevent another train robbery, and most definitely prevent injury to crews or passengers, Reed and Jackson were assigned to patrol the area around the mountain paths suspected of the gang's route to disappearance.

Scouting one of the suspicious areas between two mountains revealed evidence of activity through the canyon that lay between them. The agents located a strategic spot on the edge of a cliff, which would provide a clear view of the entrance and exit and any activity that might occur within. It allowed them quick access from their position while providing sufficient cover.

Patience and determination were qualities shared by Reed and Jackson. They were relentless when it came to stalking and capturing a criminal.

It was only a matter of time until one member of the gang was spotted. Probably sent for supplies, he appeared totally unaware and unconcerned that the location of their hideout might have been discovered, and he took his time meandering out of the canyon.

One at a time, members of the gang came through the mountain path. Each sent to find the others, or to discover what happened to them, why they hadn't returned with supplies.

Captured and in handcuffs, tied to a tree, waiting to be taken to jail, the entire ruthless gang was methodically rounded up without the firing of a single shot.

Completing the last assignment of many, Reed and Jackson turned the unsavory bunch over to the Marshal in Lawton, Oklahoma.

On their way out of town, they stopped by Miss Cheri's Millinery Shop and Home Goods Store to say hello and goodbye to the Ayers. It was discovered that the name had been changed to Ayers Dry Goods Stores, and that Cheri and Eli had two shops now, and another scheduled to open soon.

Reed and Jackson rode out of Lawton for the last time that day, and off to west Texas, where they planned to spend their retirement out near San Solomon Springs. They had bought a ranch out there a few years back. There were some peach trees on the ranch and some canals running from the springs that furnished water to the trees.

Also out there on the ranch was the grave and the marker of an old friend.

Chapter Sixty

It was a big bundle that was stuffed into the post office box. It almost took up all the space. Sara knew it was the mail collected by B.G. and Joseph Steven, mixed in with the other mail. She was anxious to get home to see the contents, see the catalogs or advertisements that might offer some items for the new shop, to see if there were any letters.

Sara kept looking at the bundle while it lay in the seat beside her. There were errands to run for the shop, and a few groceries to pick up. Her outing took much longer than intended.

The Women's Suffrage Association meeting was at noon, a function she would never miss. Sara had no patience for apathy and played a significant role for the group in the island city. She also had her own special interest in participating. The founding of the women's center was underway and she wanted to be represented at every meeting.

She was scheduled to meet with the architect and the builder who were in charge of the construction of the building on Tremont Street. The design had to be done purely from Sara's memory. She was pleased, so far, but was keeping a close eye that her recent changes were being made as planned. The architect had interpreted her thoughts very well. The construction was going well, too.

An encounter on the street with a neighboring merchant detained her even longer. When she finally got back to the shop with the mail, she was interrupted by a local artist asking to display some of his pieces at the shop, then by the policeman who stopped by each day. The mail was left on the counter.

It was Saturday, so the shop was busy all day. It seemed that even though the weather was cooler, the up-coming holidays brought people to the island. Sara and Etta were both relieved when it was finally time to close the store and lock up for the night.

Sara had to go back downstairs to retrieve the bundle. Tired and distracted by the busy day, it had been forgotten.

She sorted through the loose mail while eyeing the big bundle. Her curiosity and eagerness to examine its contents earlier in the day had waned with busy distractions. *You are going to have to wait until tomorrow.* She picked it up, tossed it back on the table, and went to bed.

Morning came early for Sara and Etta, both hungry from going to bed without dinner or much of anything for lunch. The smell of coffee and frying bacon filled the apartment, prompting Sara to join Etta in the kitchen. They shared kitchen and household duties. The positions of employer and employee had long ago faded to loving friendship.

Etta was getting older. Never in good health anyway, her movements had become slower and she was more forgetful. Sara had made a silent pledge to care for Etta until the very last.

Overnight, a heavy fog had settled in to stay. It was not unusual that time of year. Although the sounds of the surf were ever-present, the water wasn't visible, even from the short distance across the boulevard.

Because of the lack of daylight, Sara altered their usual morning routine of setting items outside on the walkway, and for safety, postponed unlocking the doors for business. She left the lights inside turned low and the closed sign on the door. Life on the island was often altered when the fog was so heavy. This day was no different than many other days that season.

The slow morning jogged Sara's memory about the bundle of mail. She hurried upstairs, snatched it off the table, and hurried back down, opening the bundle as she went. One piece at a time, sorting it into piles of similar pieces, catalogs, invoices, advertisements, letters. *Could it be? I know this handwriting.* Sara ripped open a letter.

Etta very nervously nodded her head toward the front windows. "Look outside!" She quietly brought Sara's attention to a frightening figure that was lurking around the door. Sara rang up the police. She and Etta gathered themselves behind the counter, both fearful that the figure was going to break into the store. He approached the door, peering inside, leaning from side to side, and finally, began knocking on the door. Just at that moment several policemen appeared through the fog and grabbed him. Sara hurried to the front of the store, with the letter in hand, to get a closer look. She began to recognize the outline of a slouch hat and a familiar silhouette. Suddenly, she knew that dark frightening figure that had been lurking in the fog. She grabbed the knob and flung open the door.

"Dodge!"

Chapter Sixty-one

The newspaper accounts of the war seemed more horrendous as each day passed. Now a British liner with over a thousand people aboard had been attacked and sunk off the coast of Europe. Many of those on board the ship were Americans. Most Americans and politicians had hoped to stay neutral in the war, but the attitude toward the Germans was changing rapidly. The atrocities were getting worse each day.

While the politicians argued over whether to involve the country in the war, public opinion continued to grow in favor of helping the allies. Many youth took up the cause and went to volunteer or enlist, some even going to Canada, where there were fewer questions about age.

Joseph Steven and his best friends, Lee and Richard, had been delivering and spreading pamphlets and information about war bonds when they came upon an even better idea; they would join the military and go help the allies.

Fearless and innocent youth, being the powerful thing it is, aided them in making their decision and deceiving their parents. A plan was devised whereby they would announce they were going on a camping trip. Rather than actually going camping, they would hop a freight train and make their way to Canada to join the armed forces there. Once in Canada, they would write a letter to their parents, explaining their decision and passion to help the allies, and to assure them that they needn't worry. They agreed that their parents needed to know what they had done. The three of them copied the other's letters, each assuring their parents that all would be well and they would return as soon as the war was over.

Their enlistment was welcomed in the Canadian military. They were assigned to a unit and began their training right away. The training was rigorous and intense, but brief, as the need in Europe was urgent. They remained firm in their commitment, although when it came time to ship out, many of those who had enlisted in the Canadian military and had been accepting the pay, left when it came time to ship out.

The original army was small but grew quickly. Joseph and his friends found it interesting that they had ended up serving the English Crown after their studies in history class about the American Revolution.

Grateful that they had remained together in the same unit, they pledged to protect each other, especially after they arrived at the front and saw the horrors of the bloody trenches.

Shoulder to shoulder with English and French soldiers, they shared their relief when news finally came of American forces arriving in numbers of 10,000 a day to support them.

The noise in the trenches was deafening. Joseph wished the ringing in his ears would stop, but it never let up, even when the bombs weren't exploding around him. Barbed wire in twisted rolls ran along between the trenches. Whenever there was an attempt to advance, soldiers would often get tangled in the wire or get shot or hit by shrapnel while they were running between the trenches, winding their way through the rolls of wire, tripping or falling into it. It was horrible to watch a fellow soldier or buddy, alive, being hit again and again, his body finally lifeless and dangling in the wire.

The most relentless fighting came shortly after the arrival of the American troops. Still unable to move forward, the shelling went on for days. Then one morning at daylight the shelling stopped. The sudden silence was louder than the bombs and shelling. The German offensive had finally been turned back. They lost their stronghold and finally had no more replacements. After one hundred intense days a truce was called. The war ended.

In the severity of that ongoing battle, Joseph had gotten separated from his friends. As soon as the shelling stopped, he eagerly began to search for them, running through the trenches from one end to the other, running out and about above the trenches, finally finding first Richard, and then his other friend, Lee, both dead.

The loss of his friends left a painful, numbing void in Joseph's heart. They had been his buddies for a long time, being some of the few students who had accepted him when he moved from the country to the school in Austin. They had studied together, played baseball and football together, fished and kayaked in the river, and gotten into plenty of mischief. Now they were both gone. Seeing them dead, along with other terrible sights, haunted his thoughts and dreams. He had nightmares and could hear the bombs, the artillery, the screams of wounded soldiers, and he saw the mangled bodies of his dead friends, over and over and over.

He hardly slept at all, didn't allow himself to go to sleep, and dreaded nighttime. He hadn't been shot or blown up. He still had all his limbs, no cuts, not even a bruise. His wounds were invisible, but very real.

At the end of the long voyage across the Atlantic Ocean back to Canada, he made his way through the city to the train station and boarded a train headed for Texas. He left an address for his discharge papers and never looked back.

He hadn't written to his parents or had an opportunity to write to them since he had left for Europe. He wondered if the parents of his friends had received the notification of their deaths. He was ridden with guilt that he was the only one to survive, and he was feeling very much alone.

The days of Joseph's fearless youth were over. Gone was his innocence in just a few short months that seemed like a lifetime. He made a decision to honor his parents' wish to do something meaningful with his life, to get a good education. He resolved to commit the rest of his life to them and to the memory of his friends who lost their lives in World War I.

Chapter Sixty-two

Ayers Exploration bought up oil and gas leases all over Oklahoma and the Texas Panhandle. The legal and geological teams had carte blanche as far as their board of directors was concerned. The chairman, Dodge Ayers, was a little more reserved, however, feeling that honey was better than vinegar. He didn't like that the business of oil and gas had become so competitive and sometimes ruthless.

His resources were spread among many types of businesses from retail to corporate oil and gas. For the most part he had little interest in the exploration side of the business. If not for discovering oil and gas on much of their own land, which put him right in the midst of it, they would still only be in the dry goods business. Of course, that would have made his mother happy.

His dad didn't like any of the businesses at all. He preferred staying at the ranch all the time, and did so. Of course, he was pretty feeble, so it was just as well that he was happy out there. Dodge Ayers went out to check on his dad, Eli, at least once a week, if not more. His dad had worked hard, right alongside his mother, making the stores a success, beginning with the very first one. As soon as they bought the ranch, that was over. He started staying out there all the time. It reminded him of his younger days, being out there with the horses, cooking outside, napping on the porch. He had lived most of his life out of doors, on the frontier. He camped out by the river most of the time, weather permitting. The hired help kept an eye out for him in Dodge's absence.

Being an only child with no one to share the burden of the business anymore, made his life too busy. It was all a lot more fun when his mother was alive and well. She loved each and every store and would have visited every single one of them every day if it had been physically possible. Until she got sick, she spent all her time in the stores, reluctant to trust anyone to do everything to her liking.

The one thing they could never agree on was keeping the millinery departments. They lost money trying to keep hats and gloves, when few ladies wore them anymore. The departments were still there, though. Now that she was gone, he wanted them there. Funny thing, they had begun to sell those items again.

The board had decided to venture further into Texas as far as the Texas Hill Country. The geology group had determined that there was plentiful natural gas available. Planning for a pipeline was underway. A team was already in the area running tests and visiting with landowners about more leases.

Although Dodge Ayers knew that he had roots in a little community nearby, he'd never gone there. He knew that was where his mother originally met his real dad. There had been a lot of history between those two. His mother had shared most of it with him. She felt she needed to explain when he received a letter from an attorney in Galveston about an inheritance from his uncle Dodge Blackburn, who, it turned out, was not his uncle at all, but his father. He barely remembered meeting him when he was very young, although letters and gifts came on every birthday and Christmas. His mother told him that she was certain Eli knew, although she never had told him and he never mentioned it. Cheri did not go into the details about her life before Dodge, although she did share the story about her best friend Rosie, and of course, about how Dodge Blackburn had saved her from the Indian renegade, Maw'wat.

Dodge had been all over the world, but had never been to the Hill Country in Texas. It was time to go. He instructed his secretary and one of the lawyers on the legal team to locate the little community and the encampment by Sandy Creek and to make arrangements with the owners for him to visit there. They were all going to be down there anyway. He may as well go along for the ride. After all, the owners were family, indirectly, if only through inheritance.

Dodge knew that there was no one living there anymore, like many other small communities and towns that died away as the railroads and highways bypassed them. His mother didn't know much about it, only that Dodge Blackburn had lived and worked there, but after learning about his real father, he'd made inquiries about it. He knew that everyone had left and that a rancher's son who left had come back years later and bought up all the land. His Uncle Dodge and Aunt Sara, who had owned the hotel and general store, had kept up correspondence with that family and with his own parents. They had all long since passed away. He knew that Aunt Sara's fortune was left to Joseph Steven, the same as his own inheritance came from Uncle Dodge.

Uncle Dodge had died of tuberculosis, and Aunt Sara died in her sleep within a few weeks of his death. It was just a matter of time before his father, Eli, would pass as well.

Those thoughts and plans were still in his head when his secretary interrupted to transfer a call. It was his father's caregiver. They found him early that very morning on his cot on the porch. Eli Ayers had died in his sleep.

The trip to Texas was postponed for the service, but Dodge felt more strongly than ever the need to go to the place where he knew he had roots. To see it, to feel it like his mother had described it.

Tracing the routes of which his father often spoke interested him, as well. The tales of his many trips to Texas and Oklahoma held some fascinating events. One in particular was about one of his earlier trips when he guided a party all the way to Austin, Texas from Tennessee. Most interesting was the incident at Gleason's Crossing, where a gang of white men pretended to be Indians. Dodge found those stories to be disturbing, as he was an advocate for the Indians in Oklahoma. He had found the government treatment of them throughout the state's history to be deplorable; the broken treaties, taking their land and homes, forcing them to move to the worst land imaginable, where there was no wildlife, nor decent land to farm.

Without a family of his own, Dodge chose to spend his time and resources to improve the lives of the children on the reservations. It was an interesting outcome, considering how much his mother and father hated the Indians.

His father, Eli, told him about being shot in the leg with an arrow and the infection that set in almost costing him his leg. He was scouting for a cavalry unit at the time. That was earlier days, when the Indians were still resisting the reservations. Eli lived long enough to see both sides of the Indian situation. He saw how the government broke the treaties and split up the reservations with no regard for the Indians.

His mother, Cheri, felt the same as his dad, but continued to hold onto her hate. She watched as a band of drunken Indians raped and murdered her best friend, knowing she would be next, only to be saved by his Uncle Dodge.

He was glad he went to visit the Hill Country. It was beautiful country, with creeks and rivers running through it everywhere. Seeing the area where the little community once thrived made an impression. It was sad to think that at one time it had held so much promise for the people who came there, so many hopes and dreams.

Some of the names in the cemetery were familiar. He recognized the last name, Steven, and felt sad for the parents who lost all those babies. *I guess that was Joseph Steven's family,* he thought.

Dodge turned and looked at the creek nearby. *Sandy Creek, oh the stories you could tell.*

Chapter Sixty-three

LeAnn and Elise always looked forward to summer vacation at their grandfather's ranch. They loved riding their horses and exploring. They especially enjoyed the evenings, gathering around listening to the stories about how their family came to Texas and settled in the little unnamed community nearby.

Although it was a cattle ranch, Grandpa was fond of horses and had given each of the girls a horse. When the girls were at the ranch it was their responsibility to take care of their horses. LeAnn's horse was named Rocky. Elise had chosen the name Pebble, after a horse her great-great grandmother rode and loved. Her grandpa told her about the horse among other stories of their ancestors and the old days.

When Grandpa was a child, his grandmother, Johanna, told him about her life, including her horse, Pebble. She had kept a journal for most of her life. It had been passed to his father, who had made notes in it over the

years, and then passed on to him. He took every opportunity to share the stories with his granddaughters.

Among their favorites were the ones about the
long wagon trip from Tennessee to Texas, about crossing
the Mississippi River and following along the old Shawnee
Trail. The girls studied history at school, so they especially
loved hearing how their own family settled and survived in
the early days of Texas. They enjoyed hearing how their
great-great grandfather worked for a rancher and actually
trailed one of the last cattle drives out of Texas, and how
he had to kill and bury all of his own cattle and give up his
ranch because of anthrax. They fantasized about the romance that their great-great grandmother wrote about in
her journal, how she and B.G. fell in love and married.

The very land on which their grandfather's ranch
now spread was made up in part by the small ranch that
once belonged to his grandparents. Over the years a few
other small ranches and farms were added. Grandpa's father, Joseph Steven, bought all that land because he was
determined to regain his father's original ranch. He had
become a research scientist studying diseases that afflict
livestock. A large inheritance from an old family friend,
Sara Blackburn, enabled him to create his research facility
and buy the land. Long since shuttered, his old abandoned
laboratories were still there on the ranch.

Joseph Steven and his grandson, Joseph III lost
their lives when the private plane in which they were flying

a research mission crashed there on the ranch. The girls were babies at the time.

Grandpa had done everything possible to preserve their family heritage and to share it with the girls. There was even the old newspaper article about the plane crash, framed and included in the collection at the museum, as well as many of their family artifacts. He took the girls there so they could see and learn more about their family history. They were always interested to learn more.

Many items had been passed down through the years, but the oldest and most treasured were the partial remains of the old china set that belonged to their great-great grandmother, Johanna. It had originally belonged to their ancestors from Germany. During the family move to Austin, one of the boxes disappeared. It was never recovered. That was a very long time ago, but Johanna had written in her journal how heartbroken she was at losing it, after having spent so many years trying to preserve it. What remained of those fragile old dishes were never used, but were proudly displayed in a dining room cabinet behind glass doors.

When the county museum endeavored to document the historical significance of a blacksmith shop, the family was happy to oblige by furnishing the anvil, bellows, tongs, hammers and files left from Guenther Gurganis' blacksmith shop. His name and his daughter's, Johanna

Gurganis Steven, were both on the plaque as contributors, although they had passed away long ago.

Great-grandfather Joseph was the only surviving child of four children born to his mother, Johanna. The graves of his siblings were in the little cemetery over near the old creek bridge.

In the cabinet displaying the china dishes sat an old tintype of B.G. and Johanna. The journal revealed, many times over, how hard their life was and how much they must have loved each other.

A favorite activity of the girls was to saddle up early in the morning and go for a ride. They always explored the ranch, but they particularly enjoyed visiting the clearing where the little community used to be. There had been a general store and hotel that had been demolished and hauled away, leaving scant evidence of a foundation. Their great-great-great grandfather Guenther's blacksmith shop was evidenced by a pile of rubble grown over by weeds, but was still there, after all those years. It was sad that it hadn't been cared for and preserved, but it fell down long before the family came back. There had been a rock church and school, but only the stones remained. The roof had caved in and the doors were long gone. The old cistern had been filled in and covered with stones. Remnants of the old bridge were still in the creek beside a newer, better bridge. Not too far away was evidence of another old bridge that had collapsed and washed downstream. Those old roads and bridges were now on private property and had long since been bypassed by the highway that was barely a mile over the hill.

The girls decided to see how far they could ride toward the mouth of the creek. It widened and was very shallow in most places. It wasn't more than a few feet deep even at its deepest, but that day it was little more than a trickle as water levels had dropped very low in spite of hard rains a few months back.

The girls split apart and rode along the edges of the creek. They had ridden from the new bridge, beside the old cemetery, toward the old bridge that had washed away. Grandpa had told them there used to be a swimming hole up there, so they hoped to find it. A swimming hole would be great fun.

Surprised by something she saw at the edge of the water, Elise called out to her sister. "Hey, LeAnn, come look!"

There, glistening in the sunlight just beneath the surface of the water, were shiny pieces of the china dishes, the pattern washed away by time, hardly distinguishable. They were strewn among the splintered fragments of an old sun-bleached wooden box that had been preserved in the sand, along the banks of Sandy Creek.

The End

Local Scientist Killed in Crash
Single Engine Plane Explodes On Impact

Local zoologist, Joseph Steven, PHD, and his grandson, Joseph Steven III both died when a single engine plane, belonging to Steven's Laboratories, LLC, crashed yesterday evening with both men on board. It is reported by witnesses that the plane began to lose altitude when smoke started pouring out of the engine. The accident is still under investigation.

Dr. Steven, a zoologist and veterinary pathologist, was born and raised on the ranch where the accident occurred. A landing strip and airplane hangar are located on the ranch. Joseph Steven III was the licensed pilot for Steven's Laboratories. His office and residence are also located on the ranch.

Doctor Steven leaves behind his only son, Joseph Steven II.

Joseph Steven III leaves behind his wife, Cassie, and their two young children.

Funeral arrangements are pending.

Dr. Steven's recently published research papers have been a topic of controversy, studying the effects of drought conditions on anthrax spores. There has been concern among local residents about the security at the laboratories, whether it is sufficient to protect the public.

It is reported that regulatory authorities have been notified and are in route to the laboratories to inspect and eliminate any danger that may be present.

About The Author

 Mollie Bickle Cardwell's mother and grandmother lived many of the stories told within the pages of *Return to Sandy Creek.*

The highways and by-ways of the Texas Hill Country, from San Angelo to Houston, are home to this fourth generation Texan. It was along one of those highways, during a long drive to San Angelo, that her novel began to unfold. As her retirement from a career in banking approached, the story continued to grow and the characters came to life.

A move to the area where her husband's ancestors had owned and lost a ranch near Sandy Creek brought her story full circle.

There is no end to history, so there is no end to *Return to Sandy Creek.* Families do go on, as do their memories and stories, often crossing the same paths as their ancestors.

CPSIA information can be obtained
at www.ICGtesting.com
Printed in the USA
FFOW03n1327290514
5587FF